# ALSO BY TIM HARRIS

*Mr. Bambuckle: Rule the School*

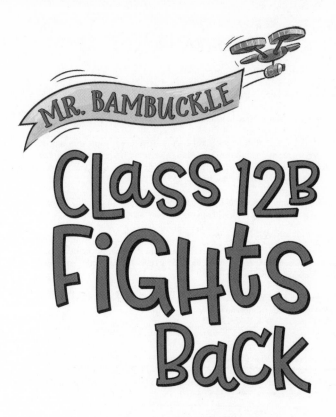

MR. BAMBUCKLE

# CLaSS 12B FiGHtS BacK

## TIM HARRIS

ILLUSTRATED BY

## JAMES HART

sourcebooks
young readers

First published in the United States in 2019 by Sourcebooks, Inc.
Copyright © 2018 by Tim Harris
Cover and internal design © 2019 by Sourcebooks, Inc.
Cover art by James Hart
Illustrations © 2018 by James Hart

Sourcebooks and the colophon are registered trademarks of Sourcebooks, Inc.

All rights reserved. No part of this book may be reproduced in any form or by any elec-tronic or mechanical means including information storage and retrieval systems—except in the case of brief quotations embodied in critical articles or reviews—without permission in writing from its publisher, Sourcebooks, Inc.

The characters and events portrayed in this book are fictitious or are used fictitiously. Any similarity to real persons, living or dead, is purely coincidental and not intended by the author.

All brand names and product names used in this book are trademarks, registered trade-marks, or trade names of their respective holders. Sourcebooks, Inc., is not associated with any product or vendor in this book.

Published by Sourcebooks Young Readers, an imprint of Sourcebooks Kids.
P.O. Box 4410, Naperville, Illinois 60567–4410
(630) 961-3900
sourcebookskids.com

Originally published in 2018 as *Mr Bambuckle's Remarkables Fight Back* in Australia by Random House Australia Children's, an imprint of Penguin Random House Australia. This edition issued based on the paperback edition published in 2018 in Australia by Random House Australia Children's, an imprint of Penguin Random House Australia.

Library of Congress Cataloging-in-Publication data is on file with the publisher.

Source of Production: Versa Press, Inc., East Peoria, IL, USA
Date of Production: March 2019
Run Number: 5014626

Printed and bound in the United States of America.
VP 10 9 8 7 6 5 4 3 2 1

RO455782978

FOR DAD

# The Students of Room 12B

## EVIE NIGHTINGALE

**likes** bright lights, open spaces, hugs

**Dislikes** being scared, basements, washing machines

## SCARLETT GEEVES

**likes** editing photos, asking questions, her favorite red ribbon

**Dislikes** too much cheese on pizza

## SAMMY BAMFORD

**likes** sports, skydiving, passing notes

**Dislikes** typos, the government, getting into trouble

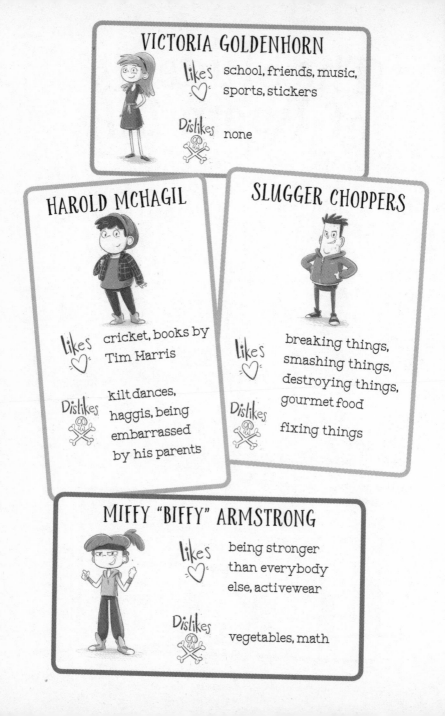

# VICTORIA GOLDENHORN

**likes** ♥ school, friends, music, sports, stickers

**Dislikes** ☠ none

# HAROLD MCHAGIL

**likes** ♥ cricket, books by Tim Harris

**Dislikes** ☠ kilt dances, haggis, being embarrassed by his parents

# SLUGGER CHOPPERS

**likes** ♥ breaking things, smashing things, destroying things, gourmet food

**Dislikes** ☠ fixing things

# MIFFY "BIFFY" ARMSTRONG

**likes** ♥ being stronger than everybody else, activewear

**Dislikes** ☠ vegetables, math

## DAMON DUNST

**likes** Victoria Goldenhorn, photos of Victoria Goldenhorn, thinking about Victoria Goldenhorn

**Dislikes** anything without Victoria Goldenhorn

## REN RIVERA

**likes** detecting, spying, living next door to Vinnie

**Dislikes** teachers who whisper in huddles

## VINNIE WHITE

**likes** curling her hair, surprises, living next door to Ren

**Dislikes** homework

## ALBERT SMITHERS

**likes** applied physics, chemical engineering, incredibly difficult math books

**Dislikes** lack of cheese on pizza

**CARROT GRIGSON**

Likes: living with Pop, feeding his pet pigeon

Dislikes: annoying ads on television

**MYRA KUMAR**

Likes: telling jokes, the internet, making money

Dislikes: boring people

**VEX VRON**

Likes: cars

Dislikes: almost everything except cars

**PETER STRAYER (ABSENT)**

Likes: absent on day of survey

Dislikes: absent on day of survey

# 1

## Miss Frost

**M**iss Frost's first day at Blue Valley School was a remarkably horrible day. The fifteen students of room 12B entered the classroom after the bell to find their new teacher listing rules on the board. Although her handwriting was stylish, the message in her perfectly-shaped words was anything but pleasant. Dreadful warnings such as "no speaking," "don't be lazy," and "there will be severe punishments" quickly filled the board. As the students took their seats, the briefest smile flickered across Miss Frost's face before she dumped eleven pages of handwriting worksheets on each of their desks.

The students looked from the worksheets to Miss

Frost with hesitation and mistrust. Her teaching methods, it appeared, were without comparison to the class's previous teacher. In his short time in room 12B, Mr. Bambuckle had completely and utterly charmed the students with his surprising tricks and fantastical lessons.

Despite her icy disposition, Miss Frost—in her sleek, wintry ensemble—was beautiful to look at. Her long, silver hair was brushed neatly into a high bun that she secured with a diamond bobby pin. The diamond glinted and glimmered in the light. Her eyes were deep gray-blue, and the students soon discovered that a single stare from their new teacher would send frightful shivers down their spines. They feared her from the get-go.

"Hey, new teacher, what's your name?" said Vex Vron, a dark-haired boy who dared to poke danger with a stick.

Miss Frost paced silently to the

back of the room where Vex sat and tapped a fingernail on his desk. "You speak with such little respect... I pity your type." Her voice was nothing more than a whisper, though very much in command.

Vex scowled. "Whatever."

Miss Frost lingered briefly at Vex's desk, her icy stare forcing him to look away. "Such a troubled child," she sniffed. She walked back to the front of the room and picked up a marker, adding another rule to the board.

> Any student who speaks out
> of turn from this point on
> will write two hundred lines
> at lunch. Discipline is the
> new order.
> -Miss Frost

Overcome by fear, the students in room 12B began working on their handwriting worksheets in silence. The only sound was Evie Nightingale chewing her fingernails. Evie was a small girl, and today, she was feeling even smaller.

Miss Frost moved stealthily around the students as they wrote.

"What a ghastly *K*."

"Have you never heard of sharpening your pencil?"

"Your *G*s are atrocious."

"Your pencil grip is as poor as your attitude."

"Do that beastly *W* again seventy-five times."

Miss Frost stopped at the desk of Victoria Goldenhorn, a girl whose handwriting was as immaculate as her long, blond hair. The teacher's lips twitched as she inspected Victoria's work. She couldn't fault it, and she didn't like the feeling of not being able to criticize. She tightened her lips and moved on to the next desk.

"Who sits here?" said Miss Frost, pointing to an empty chair.

Not one of the students was willing to risk an answer for fear of saying something wrong.

Miss Frost repeated the question, her whisper putting goosebumps on Evie Nightingale's arms. "I expect an answer. Where is this student?"

The room was silent.

"If you students had a brain between you, you would know when to speak and when not to."

Nobody spoke.

"You there." She pointed to an orange-haired boy on the other side of the classroom. "Who is missing today?"

"Peter Strayer," said Carrot Grigson, owner of the orange hair. In an attempt to soften the mood, he added, "I like your bobby pin."

Miss Frost glared at Carrot. She raised a hand and gently touched the sparkling diamond with her fingertips. For a moment, she looked as though she was lost in thought, but she soon snapped out of it. "You will never,

*ever*, under any circumstance, mention my bobby pin. Not today, not tomorrow, not ever."

Carrot gulped.

Miss Frost lowered her hand and stared fiercely at Carrot. "To ensure you get the message, see me at lunch for detention."

Carrot gulped again. Louder this time.

"Let that be a warning to all of you," said the teacher. "Anyone who mentions my bobby pin—or shows any disrespect, for that matter—can join me at lunch."

Damon Dunst, who had a strong sense of humor and wanted nothing more than to impress Victoria Goldenhorn, longed to say, "Miss Frost, will you pay for my meal if I join you for a lunch date?" He thought better of it and kept quiet.

With the students in room 12B frightened into submission, Miss Frost went back to prowling in search of a handwriting error.

"Sit up straighter, or you'll become a hunchback."

"Rewrite that *Z* until it is perfect."

"Your capital letters are disgraceful."

It was not until five minutes before morning recess that one of the students dared to put their hand up and speak. It was Victoria Goldenhorn.

"What could you possibly want, young lady?" said the teacher.

Victoria smiled and politely held up her work for inspection. "Do you think my handwriting deserves a sticker?"

Miss Frost moved closer to examine the work. "A sticker?"

"Yes, please, Miss Frost. Or a stamp. If it's okay with you, of course."

The teacher whisked the work out of Victoria's hands and scanned it carefully, her lips twitching irritably. "I know students like you," she said. "You think you are so much better than everybody else."

Damon Dunst sensed an attack on his sweetheart.

While fear had silenced him all morning, his obsession with Victoria was enough to pry open his mouth. "That's not very nice!"

Miss Frost's cold eyes shot arrows at Damon. They weren't the kind of arrows Cupid might shoot. These were arrows meant to cause pain.

Damon's face turned white.

"You rude child," Miss Frost said quietly. "I'll show you 'not very nice.'"

She held Victoria's work up for everyone to see, and then, ever so slowly, she tore it in two. Then she tore the halves in two. She continued tearing until the handwriting sheets resembled confetti. But there would be no celebration today. The relationship between teacher and students could not be worse.

Victoria's usual positivity dissolved as a single tear streaked down her cheek. She had taken a great deal of care on her handwriting.

"Like I was saying," said Miss Frost. "I know

students like you, and you need to be brought down a notch or two."

"She was only asking for a sticker," said Damon quietly.

"Silence!" snapped the teacher. It was the first time she had raised her voice.

Evie Nightingale started shaking with fear.

"As for the stickers and stamps," said Miss Frost, lowering her voice back to a frightful whisper, "where can I find the treacherous things?"

Victoria pointed feebly to the desk where Mr. Bambuckle had kept them.

Miss Frost left the shredded paper on Victoria's desk and walked to the front of the room. "No morning recess until

you've done the whole assignment again—more neatly this time."

Victoria, who had never before been so cruelly treated, sobbed silently as the teacher rummaged through the drawers of Mr. Bambuckle's desk.

"These stickers are sickening," said Miss Frost. "Who would write such ridiculous things?"

The students tried not to remember the time when Mr. Bambuckle had asked them to design new stickers. They tried not to remember the trust he had put in them. They tried not to remember the fun they had shared. Thinking about such things would only make them more upset.

Miss Frost tossed the stickers and stamps into the garbage can and turned to the class. "These hideous

things are never to be spoken of again. Discipline is the new order."

With that, she lowered a match into the steel can and set the stickers on fire.

The new teacher was quickly making her mark in room 12B, and not even the heat from the fire could warm the mood of the students. All the while, Vex Vron watched from his seat at the back of the room, his mind churning with thoughts and ideas. He was determined to ensure the return of Mr. Bambuckle, and it was time to put his plan into action.

# 2

## Totes Be Careful

If the students thought the first session with their new teacher was bad, they were in for a shock after morning recess when the principal, Mr. Sternblast, followed Miss Frost into the classroom.

Mr. Sternblast had been in some foul moods lately. The children believed he was taking pleasure in some final outbursts before his imminent departure. Rumor had it he was about to leave Blue Valley School for a higher-paying job in the city. It seemed that by firing Mr. Bambuckle, he had proved his leadership skills and earned himself a promotion.

"Listen up, class," he snapped. "I need to discuss a

few important matters with your teacher. You should all shut up and read."

The students in room 12B, whose spark had already been squashed, reached silently for their books.

Mr. Sternblast nodded in approval toward Miss Frost. "I see you already have them under good control."

Miss Frost simply straightened her skirt, demanding perfection even from the clothes she wore.

Mr. Sternblast opened a folder and began discussing school business with the new teacher. Only two students, Sammy Bamford and Carrot Grigson, dared to break the rules of silent reading.

Sammy, an athletic boy who loved to wear baseball caps, passed a piece of paper with a handwritten message to Carrot. Carrot slipped the note beneath his reading book and hastily penciled a reply.

# NOTES PASSED BETWEEN

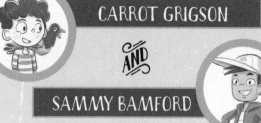

## CARROT GRIGSON

### AND

## SAMMY BAMFORD

Miss Frost isn't very nice!

Be careful. I don't want to
get caught passing notes.

She won't catch us. She's too
distracted with Mr. Sternblast.

That's even worse!

What if they BOTH catch us?!

It will be fine. Don't worry.

I certainly hope so...

Miss Frost is worse than Ms. Goss.

Yeah, the impossible has been made possible!

LOL.

You just wrote LOL but didn't laugh out loud.

Because it was funny!

But you didn't laugh out loud.

> I'm not sure that you have to
> laugh out loud when you write LOL.

Technically, you do.

Otherwise, you would write GOTI.

> What's GOTI?

Giggling on the inside.

> LOL.

You did it again!

> Did what again?

You wrote LOL without actually laughing out loud.

You're breaking the rules of the internet.

> There are no rules of the internet.

Yes, there are! Pop taught me.

> Like what?

You have to actually laugh out loud
when you write LOL.

> That's not a rule of the internet. There's
> no such thing. You're being silly, Carrot.

Miss Frost is watching us—be careful!

Miss Frost darted angry glances at Sammy and Carrot while Mr. Sternblast spoke to her. The boys were now onto their fourth piece of paper, and she was itching to punish them.

Mr. Sternblast's moustache wiggled as he tried to keep his voice down. "So that's why it will be time for me to move on."

Miss Frost nodded, her lips twitching every time she looked at Sammy and Carrot.

"Now, there are some things you should know about room 12B," said Mr. Sternblast. "It is my job to tell you before I go…"

Did you hear that? Mr. Sternblast is leaving.

I heard! But I can't believe the rumors are all true.

Miss Frost keeps looking at us.

Totes be careful.

She's the Wicked Witch of
the West.

More like the Wicked Witch of Blue Valley!
LOL.

Stop doing that! You're supposed to
actually laugh out loud. Don't break
the rules of the internet!

There are no rules of the internet!
Anyway, even if there were, they
would not recommend laughing out
loud in the same room as the Wicked
Witch of Blue Valley.

She just looked at us again.

She can look all she wants. As long as
Mr. Sternblast is talking to her, she
can't do anything.

I don't want to get caught. Please be careful,
and don't break any more rules of the internet.

For the last time, there's no such
thing!

There is—I promise!

Prove it. What's another rule of the
internet?

ROFL.

?

You can't type ROFL unless you're actually
rolling on the floor laughing.

I don't believe it! Besides, you're not
doing it now.

This doesn't count. But it's true.

It's impossible.

Why is it impossible?

You wouldn't be able to type on a
keyboard if you were rolling on the
floor laughing.

?

Think about it. Most keyboards are
attached to computers on desks.
Typing as you are rolling on the floor
laughing would mean putting the
computer on the floor with you as
you rolled around. You would probably
head butt the screen or something.

Well, you shouldn't say ROFL if you aren't going
to actually do it—even if you're writing with a
pencil and paper.

That's even worse! Can you imagine writing with a pencil while you rolled on the floor laughing?! You'd probably end up with it stuck up your nose!

What about BL?

What's that?

Belly laughing. You HAVE to be belly laughing to type or write it. Otherwise, you break the rules.

Bellies can't even laugh!

Then there's TRDMC.

Am I supposed to know what that means?

Tears running down my cheeks.

That's just depressing. Whoever types that should be focused on getting a tissue.

They could be laughing.

Rolling on the floor laughing?

ROFL—that's right!

Yay! I'm getting it. LOL.

Stop writing that without actually physically laughing out loud!!

I keep forgetting.

Miss Frost is watching us again. BRB.

Mr. Sternblast was wrapping things up with the new teacher. He was getting the impression that she was a woman very much after his own heart—someone who believed children should be whipped into shape through strict discipline.

Miss Frost listened closely to the principal. If she were to make her mark on Blue Valley School, she knew she had to make the right impression. Plus, like the principal, she had grand plans of her own. Now was the time to find out everything she could about the school.

Mr. Sternblast handed his folder to Miss Frost. "Before I go, there's one more thing I need to tell you about our routines here at Blue Valley School."

Sammy pounced on the opportunity and slid another piece of paper—the twelfth in the chain of notes—to Carrot.

> What does BRB mean?
>
> Be right back.
>
> Oooh. That makes sense.
>
> Yeah, unlike Mr. Sternblast's moustache—
> that makes no sense at all!

"Ha ha ha!" Sammy's laugh filled room 12B.

Mr. Sternblast and Miss Frost turned in fury to find the culprit.

"Oops. I probably should have written 'LOL' instead," said Sammy.

The rules of the internet had caught up with the poor boy.

"I've been watching you two passing notes," said Miss Frost, her chilling whisper impressing Mr. Sternblast. "You can't fool me."

"A sharp eye for spotting trouble," said Mr. Sternblast, nodding his balding head in approval. "And what a lovely bobby pin you're sporting, I might add."

The students held their breaths. The principal had unwittingly ventured into dangerous territory.

Miss Frost sized up Mr. Sternblast with a single glare. "With respect," she said, "you will *never* mention my bobby pin again."

The principal appeared surprised by this comment, though its steely cold delivery ensured the point was taken.

Miss Frost walked over to Sammy's desk and picked up a pile of notes. "What do you think this is?" she demanded.

"Please, don't read them," said Sammy.

There was desperation in his voice.

Carrot trembled in his chair, too scared to talk.

Miss Frost scanned the first piece of paper. Her lips remained in a thin line. "Not what I was expecting," she murmured.

This is what she read:

> THE *INDIAN SPARK-MAKER BEETLE* IS ONE OF THE RAREST INSECTS ON THE PLANET.
>
> *I DIDN'T KNOW THAT. LET'S SURPRISE OUR AMAZING NEW TEACHER, MISS FROST, WITH SOME INCREDIBLE FACTS ABOUT THE INDIAN SPARK-MAKER BEETLE.*
>
> WHAT A GREAT IDEA!

TERRIFIC! I JUST LOVE SCHOOL!

MISS FROST IS COMPLETELY BRILLIANT!

SHE KNOWS HER STUFF. HER ADVICE ABOUT
HANDWRITING IS SOME OF THE BEST I'VE
HEARD.

WE'LL HAVE TO THANK MR. STERNBLAST LATER. HE ALWAYS
HIRES SUCH WONDERFUL TEACHERS.

I LOVE HOW MR. STERNBLAST IS EXPLAINING
THE SCHOOL ROUTINES TO MISS FROST.

OUTSTANDING, ISN'T IT!

MISS FROST JUST LOOKED AT ME. SHE IS SO
BEAUTIFUL AND CLEVER—SHE EVEN KNOWS
WHEN WE'RE WRITING LOVELY THINGS ABOUT
HER!

I HOPE SHE FINDS THESE NOTES AND READS THEM. SHE
DESERVES TO KNOW WHAT WE TRULY THINK OF HER. LET'S
MEET AT THE LIBRARY AT LUNCH TO DO OUR RESEARCH ABOUT
THE INDIAN SPARK-MAKER BEETLE.

FOR SURE! THE WORLD WOULD BE A BETTER
PLACE WITH MORE MISS FROSTS IN IT.

SHE'S REMARKABLE. SHE'S SIMPLY REMARKABLE.

If Miss Frost had had her wits about her that day, she would have noticed that the handwriting on the note was much like the previous teacher's—Mr. Bambuckle.

However, in an attempt to erase all memory of the kindly teacher, she had wiped the board clean of his writing earlier that morning.

"See to it you follow instructions in the future," said Miss Frost, and for a moment, there was just a hint of cheer in her voice.

"Indian spark-maker beetle," said Mr. Sternblast to himself. "There's something familiar about that."

"Mr. Bambuckle had a—" began Evie Nightingale, her confidence briefly fueled by the memory of her favorite teacher and his mysterious pet insect.

"Silence, child," hissed Miss Frost, a single stare causing Evie to cower behind her desk.

Evie didn't speak again that day. The misery heaped upon her by the new teacher was enough to extinguish her voice altogether.

☆ ☆ ☆

Another student who was feeling entirely miserable was Scarlett Geeves. That was until she discovered a note in her schoolbag at the end of the day.

> DEAR SCARLETT,
>
> THE CLASS NEEDS YOU NOW MORE THAN EVER BEFORE.
> DON'T BE DISHEARTENED BY THE EVENTS OF TODAY, FOR
> YOU ARE ABOUT TO DISCOVER MAGIC IN YOUR FINGERS. IT
> WON'T LAST LONG, SO USE IT WISELY.
>
> MR. BAMBUCKLE

Scarlett looked around quickly in search of Mr. Bambuckle. But there was no sign of him anywhere.

She slid the note back into her bag and tightened the red ribbon in her long, black hair. While she was not sure what Mr. Bambuckle's note meant, Scarlett's whole body filled with the warmth that had been missing that day.

*I need to start keeping a diary*, she thought to herself. *Things are about to get interesting around here.*

She couldn't have been closer to the truth if she tried.

# PhotoCrop Shock

## Scarlet Geeves's Story

There really *is* magic in my fingers. Who would have thought?

Today was Miss Frost's second day with us. She has to be the nastiest person I know. She makes Cafeteria Carol look like a cuddly teddy bear, and that's saying something, especially after Cafeteria Carol chased me out of the cafeteria for not saying please.

We had a computer lesson in the library today. Miss Frost made us sit in silence. "I'm reluctant to allow you to spend time here," she said. "However, it is required by law that you learn computer skills. After this, I'll see to it that we spend the rest of the afternoon improving your handwriting."

We opened up a photo editing program called PhotoCrop. I sat next to Sammy Bamford.

He frowned at his computer and whispered under his breath. "Huh? Government override system? Who sent me this?"

Miss Frost walked past, and he quickly closed the window to avoid any trouble.

Our task was to find a photo on the internet and edit it in PhotoCrop. After some browsing, I found a photo of Blue Valley School. The photo showed the school on a bright, sunny day. The buildings reflected the sunlight like mirrors. It was a happy photo.

But I wasn't happy.

Miss Frost was making everyone feel gloomy. I wanted to show what she had done to Blue Valley School. The sunshine had left with Mr. Bambuckle.

I copied and pasted black clouds over the school. Then I added rain pouring down over every building and took away the sunny reflections in the windows. The school looked as though it was the saddest place on earth.

And that was when something strange happened.

Dark clouds suddenly filled the sky outside. It started teeming. Rain pelted against the windows.

"An unusual anomaly," observed Albert Smithers, adjusting his glasses. "It isn't supposed to rain until next week."

"Silence, Alfred," hissed Miss Frost.

"It's Albert," said Albert.

"How dare you talk back to me? That's two hundred lines at lunch."

Albert sighed and nodded.

I stared at my computer screen and then out one of the lab windows. The dark clouds over Blue Valley School looked identical to those on my screen.

I deleted a few clouds in the photo, and it got lighter outside. My heart pumped furiously, and I took my fingers off the keyboard.

I, Scarlett Geeves, could control the weather.

Next, I erased the clouds and rain altogether. In an instant, both the photo and the world outside went back to their original sunny state.

By now, even Miss Frost was peering outside. "What's going on out there?" she said, her breath misting up the window.

I was on a roll. I had to try something different.

I searched for images of fire and found a good one. It wasn't too big, but it wasn't too small either.

*Here goes nothing*, I thought to myself.

I dragged the fire across the computer screen and placed it near the bushes outside Mr. Sternblast's office.

And just like that, the fire alarm went off.

"All of you outside now," ordered Miss Frost. "We must adhere to evacuation protocol 74-C."

Despite having just been in trouble, Albert's eyes lit up at the use of such big words.

I must have been the only student who didn't look surprised by the alarm. Miss Frost glared at me with suspicion, but I quickly turned off my computer before she could see what I had done.

☆ ☆ ☆

Sometimes I wonder why Miss Frost went into teaching in the first place. All she does is work us like slaves and hand out punishments. She goes on and on about "improved grades" and "discipline."

"This writing is completely unacceptable," she said to Victoria the next day.

Miss Frost picked up Victoria's work and tore it into pieces. It was the second time she had done that to my friend.

At morning recess, Victoria was still sad.

"Try to ignore her," I said.

"It's hard to ignore when you put so much effort into your work. My desk is turning into a mountain of shredded paper."

I rested my head on her shoulder as we watched the boys play soccer. "Don't take it personally; she did it to Myra too. I've never seen Myra so upset. Well, apart from that time she dropped all her change down the drain."

Victoria took a bite from her apple and smiled, mustering some positivity.

I decided to tell her about the computer lesson and Mr. Bambuckle's note.

"*You* caused the rain?" she said. "I wondered what all that was about."

"And the fire," I added.

"But how?"

"Mr. Bambuckle," I said. "He wrote me a note to tell me there's magic in my fingers."

Victoria took another bite from her apple and listened.

"But he said it won't last long," I remembered. "So I have to use it wisely."

"Why don't you go to the computer lab at lunch-time today?" suggested Victoria. "You could test out PhotoCrop and see if it's still doing funny things."

"That's exactly what I had in mind," I said.

☆ ☆ ☆

Aside from Albert Smithers and Sammy Bamford, the computer lab was empty.

Albert had finished his lunch early and was research-ing something about metaphysics online. He was often looking into stuff that even our teachers didn't know anything about.

Sammy was watching sports videos, but he kept glancing around suspiciously, mumbling something about a government override system.

The librarian, Mrs. Paige, was busy putting away books. Her curly hair bobbed up and down as she reached for different shelves. It would be a while before she came to check on the students in the lab.

I sat down with Victoria at a computer and opened PhotoCrop.

"What comes next?" she whispered.

"We find photos."

"Of what?"

I had already thought of that. "Check it out," I said.

I found the same photo of Blue Valley School and dropped it into PhotoCrop. Then I found a picture of a small tornado and dragged it over the school oval.

"As soon as I let go of the computer mouse," I said, "the tornado will come to life."

And that was exactly what happened.

Victoria and I ran to the nearest window to look outside.

A dusty spiral of grass clippings and children's hats filled the center of the soccer field. A tornado was skidding across the grass. Kids ran screaming in all directions.

"That's nuts!" Victoria laughed.

The magic in my fingers was well and truly alive. All I had to do was test out a few more ideas.

"Watch this," I said, dashing back to the computer.

I deleted the tornado and replaced it with a photo of a cat.

"The tornado's gone," said Victoria.

"What's gone?" said Albert, who was now distracted from his metaphysics and had joined Victoria at the window. "All I see is a bunch of hats falling from the sky…and a cat on the soccer field."

"How did a cat get—" began Victoria, but she cut herself short when she realized what I had done.

I clicked Delete, and the cat disappeared.

"Where did it go?" said Albert. He took off his glasses and blinked, rubbing his eyes. "Talk about abstract metaphysics… Maybe it's time I got some stronger lenses."

Victoria smothered her giggles.

Sammy high-fived his computer screen. "Yes! Take that, government override system!"

Mrs. Paige tapped on the door to the lab. "Is everything okay in here?"

"Just fine, thank you," said Victoria.

"I hope so," said the librarian, not entirely convinced. "I'll be putting more books away if anyone needs me."

Albert walked back to his seat, muttering something about vanishing cats and wishing that his kindergarten buddy would disappear instead.

Sammy kept tapping away at his keyboard, deep in concentration.

"Told you," I said as Victoria joined me at the computer. "There really *is* magic in my fingers."

"It's amazing," she replied. "I've never seen anything like it."

I hadn't seen anything like it either, and I thought

about the note from Mr. Bambuckle. "But I don't know what I'm supposed to do with it."

Victoria stared thoughtfully at the computer screen. "We know you can change the weather," she said.

"Yep."

"We know you can make fire."

"Yep."

"And we know you can make cats appear and disappear."

"What's your point?"

"Well," she said, her lips curling into a grin, "have you tried using it on people?"

"What do you mean?"

"Mrs. Paige. Try doing something to her."

While I could try explaining what happened next, I think I'd be better at drawing it.

Victoria and I barely managed to stifle our giggles until the bell sounded. It was the most we'd laughed since Mr. Bambuckle left.

"Do you realize what this means?" said Victoria. "If PhotoCrop works on Mrs. Paige, it must work on Miss Frost too!"

☆ ☆ ☆

The next day, before the morning bell had done its thing, I went to the library.

Mrs. Paige was busy covering some new books. She was happy to let me use the computers. "Sounds like you're working on something pretty serious," she said.

"It *is* a big project," I replied.

"I admire your hard work, Scarlett."

I paused at the door to the computer lab. "Mrs. Paige," I said, "what's Miss Frost's first name?"

Mrs. Paige was gentle but firm. "That's Miss Frost's personal information."

"It's for my project," I pleaded. "It's very important."

Mrs. Paige blinked a few times, then lowered her voice. "Well, in that case, it's Belladonna... Belladonna Frost."

"Thank you," I said.

I slipped into the lab and turned on a computer. My heart hammered against my ribs. I hadn't been very nervous when I used PhotoCrop before, but what I was about to do made me shiver with fear.

I opened an internet browser and took a deep breath, typing "Belladonna Frost" into the search engine.

One photo.

There was only *one* photo of our cold-blooded teacher on the entire internet.

I clicked on the link and enlarged the photo to get a better look.

It was a close-up head shot of Miss Frost. Her gray-blue eyes pierced the camera lens.

Poor photographer.

But I wasn't worried about that now. I was more concerned about what I would do with the photo. A million ideas bounced around in my mind like Ping-Pong balls.

My palm felt sweaty against the computer mouse. I shuddered at the thought of Miss Frost finding out what I was doing. I quickly copied the image over to PhotoCrop and placed it in the middle of the screen.

I hovered the mouse over her nose and double-clicked. Then I moved the cursor to a tab named Sizing and clicked Enlarge.

Miss Frost's nose stretched until it was three times its original size. It was hideous. It was as long as Pinocchio's but as wide as a bulldog's.

Then I did something I hadn't done in PhotoCrop before.

I clicked Save.

☆ ☆ ☆

When Miss Frost walked into class a few minutes late with an enormous bandage covering her nose, I knew what had happened.

Her whisper was laced with venom. "If any of you so much as breathes too loudly, it will be five hundred lines at lunch."

We locked eyes, and she stared straight through me. I shivered.

"I don't know what your game is," she said, surveying the room, "but when I find out who did this, I'm going to make them pay...*dearly*."

Vex smirked, trying hard not to make it obvious he was staring at the bulge beneath Miss Frost's bandage.

Evie Nightingale shrunk back in her chair, nibbling one of her fingernails the way a frightened rabbit chews on a carrot stick.

Miss Frost advanced toward Evie's desk and

towered over her. "You there... Eden, isn't it? Who did this to me?"

Evie could only quiver in reply.

"I asked you a question!" roared the teacher, losing her cool. "Respect means answering, you cowardly child!"

Poor Evie's shoulders shook as she sobbed into her hands.

Miss Frost paced the room. "Who knows who did this?" Her cold, blue eyes caught mine again. "Charlotte, isn't it?"

"Scarlett," I said as calmly as I could.

"Yes, Scarlett... Do you know anything about this?"

Victoria shot me a worried glance. She knew it was me.

I shook my head. "No, Miss Frost, I don't know anything about it."

Miss Frost's lips tightened, and she continued to prowl the room. "Mr. Sternblast warned me about this class. You've barely made any progress lately. Your last teacher, Mr. Slamtackle or whatever his name was, didn't teach you a thing."

Evie blinked away some of her tears.

"Things are going to change around here," continued Miss Frost, tapping the bandage over her nose. "From now on, you're going to learn *my* way. Discipline is the new order."

I gulped.

"If you haven't memorized your thirteen and fourteen times tables by morning recess, you'll be staying in to learn them *every* morning recess until you do."

Albert put his hand in the air.

"What is it, Alfonso?"

"I already know every times table up to 247."

"Then you'll memorize 248 and 249!" With that, she tore the bandage from her face, exposing her enlarged nose for all to see.

Everyone gasped.

Slugger Choppers passed out.

"*I've* got nothing to hide," said Miss Frost. "But I will find the individual who does."

☆ ☆ ☆

Miss Frost's warning was branded into my memory like an unwanted tattoo. I didn't feel like eating any of my morning snack.

"Lucky you're good at math," said Victoria. "At least you can escape the classroom for the time being."

"Thanks to Mr. Bambuckle," I said. "I think Miss Frost was surprised we all knew our thirteen and fourteen times tables."

"It made her angry," said Damon, who was sitting next to Victoria. "She was expecting us to fail. I think she wanted to keep interrogating us at morning recess."

Vex walked over to where we were sitting. This was strange for him. He usually preferred to play basketball or goof around on the soccer field. "Can I speak to you?" he asked, looking at Victoria.

"Me?" she replied.

"Yeah, you."

Damon's broad smile vanished. He didn't like it when other boys talked to Victoria.

"Of course," said Victoria.

Vex took Victoria far enough away so that we couldn't hear him talking. He waved his arms around as he spoke and frowned a lot.

Victoria nodded as she listened.

Vex reached into his pocket and pulled out a piece of paper. He gave it to Victoria.

"I wonder what they're doing?" I said.

"I hope he's not proposing," said Damon. "*I'm* the one who's supposed to marry her."

Vex dashed away, and Victoria walked back to where we were sitting.

"What did he want?" I asked.

"I can't say," said Victoria. "He made me promise not to tell anyone."

This upset Damon. "There should be no secrets between a man and a woman." He stood up and pounded his chest, a little like Harold does in his kilt dances. "Nooo seeecreeets!"

Victoria was patient with Damon and blinked her bright-blue eyes. "As much as I'd like to, I really can't talk about it."

Damon, realizing half the playground was watching, stopped his performance and broke into a grin. "She blinked at me!"

The bell rang, and Victoria turned to me. "Be careful in class, won't you?" she said. "Miss Frost is getting suspicious."

"I know."

"What are you going to do to her next?"

"I *do* have one more idea," I said. "But the trouble is I'll only be able to try it once."

"Oh," said Victoria.

"I just need two things to make it work."

"What two things?"

"Peter Strayer, to start with."

"But he's always absent," said Victoria.

"Exactly," I said, tapping the side of my nose slyly. "That's why he's perfect—he won't get in trouble."

"What's the second thing you need?"

"A full-body photo of Miss Frost. The only picture I can find of her on the internet is a head shot."

"Why do you need a full-body photo?"

It was my turn to keep a secret. "You'll see," I said. "Just wish me luck, because I'll only get *one* chance."

☆☆☆

The next morning, Miss Frost's warning was still fresh in my memory. I knew I had to make my move. There was a feeling deep in the pit of my stomach that time was running out to use my powers. I thought about the note from Mr. Bambuckle.

*It won't last long, so use it wisely.*

Miss Frost gave us one of her stares as we took our seats. She adjusted the diamond bobby pin in her hair and scratched her triple-sized nose, which probably should have been under a bandage.

Slugger Choppers passed out again.

"This morning, you will memorize the meaning and spelling of every word in the *A* section of the dictionary. You need to catch up on all the learning you missed with your last teacher."

Albert put his hand in the air.

"Not you again," said Miss Frost.

"I already know the *A* sec—"

"Then memorize the *B* section."

"Already done."

Miss Frost raised her eyebrows. "How about you memorize the periodic table?"

Albert shrugged his shoulders. "I know that too. Mr. Bambuckle used to let me—"

"Do not mention that man's name again!" seethed Miss Frost.

Albert jerked so suddenly that his glasses fell off his face. "It's just that he—"

"Silence!"

Albert was saved by a knock at the door. Mrs. Paige had arrived to deliver some library books.

"I'll deal with you in a moment," said Miss Frost to Albert.

Sensing the tension, Mrs. Paige tiptoed inside and placed the books on the desk at the front of the room. But before she could leave, Miss Frost whispered in her ear. Mrs. Paige nodded and pointed toward me, looking guilty as she did. Then she slinked back through the door, shaking her head at me as if to apologize.

"Scarlett Geeves," said the teacher slowly. "I believe you've been spending a lot of time in the computer labs recently."

I didn't dare answer.

"I believe you've been asking about my first name."

I couldn't have said anything even if I'd tried. My throat was too dry.

Miss Frost picked up one of the library books on the front desk. "See me at lunchtime, Scarlett. We'll discuss your punishment then."

Her voice was frostier than the coldest night, and I knew it meant big trouble.

Victoria's face drained of all blood.

"Where is Peter Strayer today?" said Miss Frost, reading the tag on the library book. "Absent as usual."

At the mention of Peter's name, I snapped into action. He was part of my plan. I pulled out my phone and took a photo of Miss Frost. It was a perfect full-body shot.

"What do you think you're doing?" she said angrily. "Give me that phone at once!"

I tried to put the phone back into my pocket, but Miss Frost was too fast. She grabbed my wrist and tried to pry the phone free.

"Let me go!" I yelled. This wasn't part of my plan.

"Not until you give me that phone!"

My wrist was hurting. Miss Frost may have been thin, but she was very strong. She forced my hand open, and the phone slid loose.

It landed on the floor.

Sammy Bamford picked it up. "Looking for this?" he said to the teacher.

"Give that to me, or you'll regret it!" demanded Miss Frost. She was becoming flustered and lunged at Sammy.

Sammy tossed the phone to Slugger.

My classmates were bravely trying to help me, but I had to get the phone back. My plan wouldn't work without it.

Miss Frost launched herself at Slugger. "You'd better delete that photo, or else!" she shrieked.

Slugger lobbed the phone to Albert, who did something brilliant. He pulled out his own mobile phone and held it next to mine. In their black cases, the two phones looked almost identical.

"I suppose you'll have to figure out which phone is Scarlett's," he said, throwing one to his right and one to his left.

The rest of the class caught on, Albert's pluckiness spurring them to action. Everyone reached for their phones and started tossing them around. It was like a giant game of hot potato or, more accurately, hot device-o.

Miss Frost jumped up and down in the center of the room. She raged and roared and flapped her arms around in an attempt to catch a phone. She was completely losing her cool.

Suddenly, I found myself holding my own phone.

I dashed outside, sprinting toward the library and praying Peter had done what I'd asked him to do.

"You're not supposed to be in here," squeaked Mrs. Paige.

I ignored her and raced past. My stomach churned. What if Peter had forgotten? There wouldn't be enough time to carry out my plan.

I charged through the doors of the computer lab.

Peter had done his job! For someone who was usually absent, he had risen to the occasion. One of the computers was turned on. He had opened up PhotoCrop and my email server. He had opened up a map of the world. He had opened up hope for the class. I sat down and unlocked my phone.

I selected the photo of Miss Frost.

I heard footsteps running into the library.

"Where is she?" boomed a voice. It was Miss Frost, and she wasn't whispering anymore.

I used my phone to send the photo to myself in an email and then logged into my inbox on the computer. *Come on, come on.* My heart was beating faster than the footsteps in the library.

Miss Frost appeared in the doorway. "I'll have you expelled for this, you horrible girl!"

*Ping!*

The photo arrived in my inbox.

Miss Frost stared at the computer. Her eyes widened at the photo of herself on the screen. "What are you doing?"

I dragged the photo of Miss Frost onto the map of the world.

"Explain yourself!"

I positioned her over a country far, far away that I didn't recognize.

She took a few more steps toward me. "EXPLAIN YOURSELF!"

I moved the mouse over the Save icon.

*Click.*

Silence.

Miss Frost was gone. She had vanished into thin air. I had PhotoCropped her out of Blue Valley.

Mr. Sternblast burst into the computer lab. "What's all this commotion? What's going on?"

I quickly switched off the computer and looked innocently at the principal.

Mr. Sternblast glanced around the empty lab. "Where's your teacher? Where's Miss Frost? Tell me immediately!"

I took a deep breath and told him the honest truth. "I don't know, sir. I don't know where she is."

# 3

## A Pleasant Surprise

**M**r. Sternblast stood in room 12B later that morning with a folder in his hands. He was frowning—which was normal for him—though this was a frown of complete confusion. "Err…I'm not sure how to say this."

The students in room 12B sat up straight in their chairs as they listened.

"Umm…" the principal stammered. "It appears as though there has been some sort of…mix-up… Yes, a mix-up."

Miffy Armstrong, the sportiest and strongest girl in Blue Valley, adjusted her headband. She leaned forward, itching to hear the news.

Mr. Sternblast opened the folder. "I just received a phone call from Miss Frost." He paused, looking around the room. Scarlett Geeves fidgeted nervously with a pencil on her desk. "It seems she has gotten herself rather lost."

Albert Smithers raised his hand.

"Yes, Smithers?"

"Where is she?"

Mr. Sternblast pulled on his moustache as he thought about the answer. He blinked quickly and replied in the quietest voice the students had ever heard him use.

"Ecuador."

Vex Vron had to bite his lip to stop himself from laughing.

Albert raised his hand again.

"Yes?" said the principal.

"How did she get to Ecuador?"

Scarlett suddenly lost control of her pencil, and it clattered to the floor.

Albert's question, meanwhile, had snapped Mr.

Sternblast back into principal mode. "That, Smithers, is a *very* good question. Nobody has been able to tell me anything…although I have my suspicions."

Scarlett turned bright red and tried not to look the principal in the eye.

Mr. Sternblast's moustache wobbled crankily. "Make no mistake, I will do everything in my power to bring that talented teacher back to this school as quickly as possible. Discipline *will* be the new order."

Miffy bravely piped up with a burning question. "Mr. Sternblast, who is going to teach us in the meantime?"

The principal turned to another page in his folder and frowned again. Though this time, it was one of frustration. "I have some regretful news."

Victoria and Vex exchanged a knowing glance. Vex did a silent fist pump under his desk.

"The school board—buffoons that they are—have chosen to reappoint your old teacher."

"Miss Schlump?" asked Miffy.

"Of course not!" said Mr. Sternblast. "They've reappointed that bumbling Mr. Bam—"

Mr. Sternblast tried to finish his sentence, but the students were already hooting and howling.

Carrot clapped loudly.

Sammy threw his hat in the air.

Scarlett danced on her chair.

Vex looked rather pleased with himself.

Damon longed to embrace Victoria, but she was too busy throwing her confetti work in the air in celebration.

The euphoria in room 12B created an energy that Mr. Sternblast was not used to. In his mind, things should be done quietly and in an orderly manner. School was about regulations, not emotions. The current scene of elation was simply too much for him. He growled and stormed out.

Just as the principal left, a unicycle wheeled itself through the door. The students hushed and held their breaths. The unicycle whizzed around Victoria's desk and rested in the corner at the front of the room. The sound and smell of sizzling bacon wafted in from outside, along with a familiar voice. "It's never too late in the morning for bacon and eggs, wouldn't you say?"

Mr. Bambuckle strode into room 12B and grinned at the students, his blue suit sparkling as brightly as ever. He was holding his frying pan, which was overflowing with breakfast.

"You're back!" cried Myra.

"We missed you!" said Harold McHagil.

"And I, you," said Mr. Bambuckle, beaming at the class. He walked around the room and held out the frying pan so the students could take some food. He paused at Scarlett's desk. "Dear Scarlett, how delightful it is to see you again."

Scarlett tightened the red ribbon in her hair. "There *was* magic in my fingers."

Mr. Bambuckle winked. "I trust you found my note, then?"

Scarlett glanced at the door to make sure Mr. Sternblast wasn't there before returning the wink and taking a piece of bacon.

The teacher made his way over to Vex's desk. "And

Vex… Vex Wilberforce Vron, your unseen sacrifice is a big part of the reason I am here today."

Vex shot another glance at Victoria. "How did you know about—"

"Remember, I know everything."

Vex's usually cool face produced a smile. It was a rare smile that warmed the hearts of his classmates.

"But I didn't do it alone," said Vex. "Victoria helped me."

"Can somebody tell me what's going on?" said Slugger Choppers. "Who did what?"

"I had a chat with my dad," said Vex. "He owns three car lots."

"So?" said Slugger. "Cafeteria Carol owns three rolling pins."

Vex raised an eyebrow and continued. "I asked Dad to offer vehicle upgrades to members of the school board if they let Mr. Bambuckle come back to teach us."

"Oh," said Slugger, shaking away thoughts of

Cafeteria Carol threatening him with a rolling pin. "Why would your dad do that? He hates giving away cars."

"Because," said Vex, "I told him I'd start working in one of his car lots if he did. And he agreed. He said it would teach me to be like him—a tough, hardworking businessman—so I can take over the company one day. There was just one problem. Dad doesn't have any contacts on the school board. That's where Victoria came in. Her dad knows someone, so I asked her to pass on the car offer."

"I remember seeing you give Victoria a note," said Damon. He gazed dreamily at his crush. "She's my hero."

"Then I suppose it came down to me," said Scarlett. "I had to figure out how to get rid of Miss Frost."

"And you did," said Mr. Bambuckle. "In a most remarkable way."

"But what if Miss Frost comes back?" said Evie Nightingale, her eyes darting around the room.

Mr. Bambuckle put the empty frying pan on his

desk. "There's far too much work to catch up on to worry about that."

Everyone cheered.

"To begin with, I would like you all to draw the most amazing cake you can imagine."

The sound of pencil cases being unzipped filled the air.

While the students talked excitedly about their favorite cakes, Mr. Bambuckle walked around the room, stopping only to speak with Sammy Bamford. "I trust you found the government override system helpful?"

Sammy's eyes widened. "You sent me those links?"

Mr. Bambuckle nodded. "Indeed, I did."

"But why?"

Mr. Bambuckle lowered his voice. "My dear Sammy, I have a feeling that certain…*hacking* skills will assist you in a moment of need."

Just as Sammy opened his mouth to reply, Mr. Bambuckle clapped his hands together. "Wonderful students, it's time to design!"

"I'm drawing a wedding cake," said Victoria. "I'm actually going to a wedding tomorrow."

"I'll be at the same wedding!" announced Damon.

"Make sure you behave, Damon," joked Carrot.

"I will," said Damon, batting his eyelashes at Victoria. "Trust me, I will."

# How to Behave Appropriately at a Wedding

## A REFLECTION BY DAMON DUNST

This guide is dedicated to the love of my life:
Victoria Goldenhorn.

♡ <u>Do:</u> Arrive a little early to make sure you get a seat.

☠ <u>Don't:</u> Arrive at precisely the same time as the bride and find yourself walking down the aisle next to her, staring lovingly into the eyes of the man at the front of the church.

♡ <u>Do:</u> Realize your mistake and allow the bride to proceed without you.

☠ <u>Don't:</u> Continue walking down the aisle next to the bride, staring lovingly into the eyes of the man at the front of the church.

♡ **Do:** Slip into the nearest seat to avoid making a complete mess of the situation.
☠ **Don't:** Make a complete mess of the situation by pushing ahead of the bride and joining the groom at the altar.

♡ **Do:** Get away from the altar!
☠ **Don't:** Take hold of the groom's hands.

♡ **Do:** Apologize and escape before the bride and groom try to kill you.
☠ **Don't:** Attempt to make up for the situation by singing a rare Mongolian welcome song to the guests.

♡ **Do:** Duck.
☠ **Don't:** Collect the groom's fist on your chin.

♡ **Do:** Remember that Victoria Goldenhorn is at the wedding and control your actions.
☠ **Don't:** Remember that Victoria Goldenhorn is at the wedding and try to impress her by punching the groom back.

♡ **Do:** Allow the bride's extended family to wrestle you away from the altar.

☠ **Don't:** Identify the bride's great-grandmother as a major threat and try to eliminate her.

♡ **Do:** Apologize to everyone and calmly take your seat.

☠ **Don't:** Do anything else.

♡ **Do:** Enjoy the ceremony and wait until the bride and groom have left the church before worrying about finding Victoria Goldenhorn.

☠ **Don't:** Snap into stealth mode during the vows and commando crawl under the church pews in search of the love of your life.

♡ **Do:** Give up when you can't squeeze between a pair of unidentifiable legs.

☠ **Don't:** Bite the legs to make them move.

♡ **Do:** Duck.

☠ **Don't:** Collect a shoe on the chin.

♡ **Do:** Retreat.

☠ **Don't:** Bite the legs again.

♡ **Do:** Stop being such an idiot, admit your fault, and commando crawl back to safety.

☠ **Don't:** Push past the kicking legs, collecting dozens of blows, because you've spotted Victoria's shoes a few rows away.

♡ **Do:** Gently tap Victoria's ankle to get her attention.

☠ **Don't:** Grab her ankle and say you'll never let go until she agrees to marry you.

♡ **Do:** Stop making a racket.

☠ **Don't:** Climb out from under the pews and announce your undying love for Victoria in front of everyone.

♡ <u>Do:</u> Sit down and shut up.

☠<u>Don't:</u> Get ushered out of the church by relatives of the bride, including her rather fierce great-grandmother.

♡ <u>Do:</u> Wait for the bride and groom to leave the church and throw confetti over them.

☠<u>Don't:</u> Wait for the bride and groom to leave the church and blast them with a powerful hose because you think water fights are fun.

♡ <u>Do:</u> Turn the hose off.

☠<u>Don't:</u> Enjoy the water fight so much you start soaking the other wedding guests.

♡ <u>Do:</u> Stop hosing once everyone is saturated.

☠<u>Don't:</u> Continue to hose the bride's

great-grandmother because you think she's a major threat.

♡ <u>Do:</u> Go home while you still have the chance.
☠ <u>Don't:</u> Invite yourself to the reception at the adjoining venue.

♡ <u>Do:</u> Mingle politely with the other guests while you wait for the bride and groom to return from their photo shoot.
☠ <u>Don't:</u> Laugh at guests who are still trying to dry their clothes.

♡ <u>Do:</u> Take a photo of the wedding cake and post it on Instantgram.
☠ <u>Don't:</u> Take a photo of yourself eating a slice of the wedding cake and post it on Instantgram.

♡ <u>Do:</u> Remember that wedding cakes are special and walk away.

☠ <u>Don't:</u> Enjoy the cake so much you have another slice.


♡ <u>Do:</u> Try and make some kind of attempt to leave the cake alone.

☠ <u>Don't:</u> Cut slices for the other guests and hand them out, giving an extra-large piece to Victoria and none to the bride's great-grandmother.


♡ <u>Do:</u> Explain to the bride and groom, who have returned from having their photos taken, that you will order them another cake.

☠ <u>Don't:</u> Explain to the bride and groom that there's only enough cake left for some slapstick comedy and thrust a slice into each of their faces.


♡ <u>Do:</u> Run for your life.

☠ <u>Don't:</u> Ever go to a wedding again. (Apart from when you marry Victoria. You can go to that one.)

# 4

# Mr. Sterncake

Victoria Goldenhorn walked into room 12B the following Monday morning, desperately fighting an attack of the giggles as she told Myra about the wedding. All it took was one glance at Damon for that battle to be lost. She was ambushed by full-belly laughter.

Damon, on the other hand, sat sheepishly at his desk, clutching his stomach. He still hadn't recovered from the generous helpings of cake he'd consumed at the reception.

Balancing gracefully on his unicycle, Mr. Bambuckle welcomed the class with a wave.

"What do you have in store for us today?" asked

Miffy Armstrong, stretching a calf muscle before she sat down.

"My dear Miffy," said Mr. Bambuckle, his green eyes sparkling, "if I told you, it would ruin the surprise!"

"I love surprises," said Miffy.

"You may recall that you designed and drew the most splendid cakes last Friday," said Mr. Bambuckle, his voice as musical as an orchestra. "It's time to share your masterpieces."

The class opened their art books. This is what they had drawn:

- Miffy's cake was decorated with sports equipment.

- So was Sammy's, but his was twice as big.

- Damon's was covered in pictures of Victoria.

- Scarlett drew a cake that looked like a giant ribbon.

 - Victoria drew a perfectly circular cake, decorated in the fanciest way possible.

- Carrot's cake was in the shape of a pigeon.

- Myra's cake looked like a hundred-dollar bill.

- Harold's cake resembled a giant haggis ball.

- Slugger's cake looked as delicate as a flower.

- Evie sketched a cake that looked like a shiny new toaster.

- Ren's cake was decorated like a detective's badge.

- Peter's cake was missing. All that remained were a few crumbs on a plate.

- Vinnie's cake was tall and thin.

- Albert's cake looked like something from a science experiment.

- Vex drew a cake of Mr. Sternblast frowning. It had too much icing, and it looked like his face was melting.

"Of course, I'm not surprised your cakes are so magnificent," said Mr. Bambuckle. "Cake is a wonderful vehicle." He winked at Victoria.

"What do you mean?" said Victoria.

"You will find out in time," said the teacher, a mischievous grin on his face.

Mr. Sternblast's head suddenly popped around the corner of the doorway. Vex hastily covered his drawing with his hands.

"Dear Mr. Principal," said Mr. Bambuckle, "do join us. We are always most thrilled to be in your dazzling company."

"Enough of the superlatives, Bambuckle." Mr. Sternblast marched to the front of the room. "I have come to address some rumors."

The students sat in silence, unsure where Mr. Sternblast was going with this announcement.

Mr. Sternblast pulled at the tip of his moustache with two fingers, and it twanged back into shape. "It has come to my attention that some of you think I am leaving Blue Valley for another school in the city."

Myra Kumar stopped sketching in her book and looked up at the principal.

Mr. Sternblast narrowed his eyes. "This is no longer true."

The students were on the edges of their seats. In their minds, the principal was as good as gone. This revelation had shattered that belief in an instant.

"I admit that another school did express interest," continued Mr. Sternblast. "However, they withdrew their offer due to...*unforeseen* circumstances."

Scarlett Geeves bit her bottom lip.

"You may be wondering why I am telling you this," said Mr. Sternblast. His voice dropped to a whisper, reminding the students of Miss Frost's arctic tone. "It would seem that certain members of this class have made an enemy out of me. And until I find out who is behind this nonsense, I'll consider you *all* the enemy."

Harold McHagil, whose hearing occasionally let him down, leaned over to Vex. "Who made anemones? I can't see any rock pools."

Mr. Sternblast exploded like a sea mine. "Your rudeness will not be tolerated! My office—now!"

Harold gulped and followed the principal out of the room.

While the students processed this shocking new information, Mr. Sternblast's words hung in the air.

*I'll consider you* all *the enemy.*

Mr. Bambuckle knew his class was rattled. He also knew they needed a break from the drama. Recent events had stretched their young minds too far into the world of adults. Recognizing that this was not a very nice place to be, the teacher clapped his hands. "I think it's time we baked some cakes."

"Where are we going to get the ingredients?" said Evie, her quiet voice regaining a little strength in the presence of her favorite teacher.

"I happen to know some people," said Mr. Bambuckle.

Before he had even finished speaking, there was a knock at the door. "Delivery for Bambuckle."

"Yes, right in here, thank you," sang the teacher.

An incredibly enormous cart, wheeled by an incredibly short man, entered the room. It was piled high with all the things necessary for cake making: flour, sugar,

butter, jam, icing, and countless other goodies perfect for decorating.

"Do tell that wonderful boss of yours I owe him one," said Mr. Bambuckle.

The deliveryman tipped his hat in reply. "No, sir, my boss says he owes *you*. He's *always* talking about his time as a student in your classroom."

Ren Rivera leaned across to her best friend, Vinnie White. "Mr. Bambuckle doesn't look old enough to have taught that man's boss."

The man tipped his hat again and left, whistling a tune that sounded much like the rare Mongolian welcome song the students had grown accustomed to.

"The million-dollar question, dear class, is who is ready for some baking?" said Mr. Bambuckle.

"Me, me, me!" replied a chorus of voices, including Harold, who had returned from the principal's office.

Mr. Bambuckle smiled at Harold. "Remember, due respect."

"June respect," said Harold, mishearing deliberately this time.

"LOL," said Sammy.

Carrot shook his head. "Good try, Sammy. You should have *actually* laughed that time."

"Oh," said Sammy, who was still trying to come to grips with the rules of the internet.

To say the students in room 12B enjoyed the next few hours that morning would be quite an understatement. Mr. Bambuckle equipped them with everything they needed to simply have fun. The worries of the world faded away, replaced by cake pans and sticky mixtures.

Mr. Bambuckle kept an especially close eye on Victoria Goldenhorn's progress. "Don't forget," he reminded her, "cake is a wonderful vehicle."

Victoria smiled, though she wasn't altogether sure what he meant.

The teacher stopped at Sammy's desk too. "And don't forget, dear boy, your little computer override trick."

Sammy hadn't forgotten, but the promise of baked deliciousness was currently more important to him—that, and trying to figure out when to laugh out loud.

"How are we going to bake fifteen cakes at once?" said Ren, holding her gooey batter up for the teacher to see. "We don't even have an oven."

Mr. Bambuckle reached into one of the pockets inside his jacket and retrieved a familiar orange bouncy ball. He threw it at the light switch, flicking the lights off. Shutters fell over the windows, blackening the room.

"How do you remember what's inside each pocket?" said Vex, his voice cutting through the dark.

The bouncy ball, now glowing in the dark, returned to Mr. Bambuckle, and he caught it.

"I'm not quite sure of that myself, dear Vex." He threw the ball at the light switch again. The lights flickered back on, and the shutters rolled away. "But what I *am* sure of is how to bake fifteen cakes."

The students in room 12B stared wide-eyed at their

desks. In front of each of them, their cakes sat steaming, as if freshly removed from an oven.

"Impossible," said Vinnie.

"Impossibly delicious!" said Carrot.

"And it will be even more delicious once you finish decorating the cakes after lunch," said Mr. Bambuckle. "Which reminds me: over lunchtime, I want you each to think of a rather ridiculous use for a cake."

# Fifteen Ridiculous Uses for a Cake

1) Freeze it until it becomes as hard as a rock and skip it across a pond.

2) Smother it all over your entire body and act the part of a zombie cake in the school play.

3) Put it in your closet for twelve weeks and then use it to investigate different types of mold.

4) Eat all the icing, then film yourself being hyperactive. Upload the video to YouToob and become an internet sensation.

5) Bake two and wear them as shoes. Actually, bake three-eat one and wear two as shoes. Or maybe eat two and wear one shoe. Mop around for a while. No, eat all three and sit down for a while. Walking is overrated. Eating cake is not.

6) Eat the cake mix before it goes into the oven. Everyone knows it tastes better that way.

7) Throw it into the air and take a photo midflight. Send the photo to the news channel and claim to have sighted a UFO.

8) Bake 5,256 cakes and use them as bricks to build a house. Note: you may need to buy a few more ovens to speed up the process.

9) Cram it into an empty bottle and sell it as "bottled cake." You never know. The idea might catch on!

10) Use it as a spongy (and rather delicious!) pillow.

11) Ever heard of a cake of soap? It's time to introduce the soap of cake! (Your skin will glow with creaminess.)

12) Bake the thinnest, widest cake in the world and wrap it around yourself like a sari.

13) Decorate it with carrots and throw a party for your pet rabbit.

14) Don't bake a cake. Buy one instead. A small one. Donate the change to the little girl singing and playing guitar at the shopping mall. This will put her in a good mood, and she'll play a happy song. The happy song will be your parents' favorite song, and they'll hear it and feel extra generous toward you. They'll raise your allowance, which will allow you to buy more cakes.

15) Bake a cake large enough to hide your little brother's birthday present–a new bike!

# Bicycle Cake

## Victoria Goldenhorn's Story

I'm not certain my idea is especially creative. I'll need some feedback from Mr. Bambuckle. It's so good to have him back with us.

At the front of the room, Mr. Bambuckle reaches into one of his jacket's inside pockets. I want to ask him about the Indian spark-maker beetle. But Albert beats me to it.

"I've read precisely seven books about insects," he says. "And yet I can't find any information on Indian spark-maker beetles. Do they really exist?"

"As sure as I'm standing here now," says Mr. Bambuckle. "But remember, they are incredibly danger-ous, so we'd best not disturb mine."

Albert nods, his eyes alight with curiosity.

Mr. Bambuckle pulls some sheets of stickers from his jacket. "When I heard about what happened to our stickers, I ordered some more."

The entire class cheers—though I cheer the loudest. Things are going back to the way we like them.

Everyone settles down and starts to decorate their cake. Mr. Bambuckle walks over to my desk. "Remember, dear Victoria, cake is a wonderful—"

"Vehicle!" I say.

"Very good," he says and smiles. "I had a feeling the idea would stick with you."

"Can I please ask you something?" I say.

"Most certainly."

"I want to surprise my brother for his birthday. I'm thinking of buying him a bike and hiding it inside a giant cake. Does this idea have wheels? I mean...not literally..."

Mr. Bambuckle's green eyes sparkle as though he has known about my plan all along. "Victoria, your idea has far greater potential than you realize. Cake can be a vehicle for...let's just say, *other* purposes."

I recognize the look on Mr. Bambuckle's face. It's the knowing look he had when he was talking to Carrot about the drone race. Something strange is going to happen. I just don't know what.

Mr. Bambuckle clicks his fingers, and a bird flies into the classroom. It lands on his shoulder. The bird has shiny blue feathers that are the same color as Mr. Bambuckle's suit.

"Is that your bird?" says Scarlett.

But Mr. Bambuckle isn't listening to Scarlett. He's

listening to the bird. He nods and whispers something we can't hear. The bird chirps brightly and flies back out of the room.

"What was that about?" asks Ren.

"Birds are marvelous creatures," says Mr. Bambuckle. "Did you know that carrier pigeons were used to relay messages in times of war?"

Carrot's face lights up. "I did! Some war pigeons have even been awarded medals for bravery!"

"Right you are, dear Carrot!" says Mr. Bambuckle. He clicks his fingers again, and the bird flies back through the window. It loops around his head and then zips to the back of the room before heading straight for one of his pockets, disappearing inside.

"You keep a bird in your pocket?" asks Ren.

"Don't you?" says Mr. Bambuckle. "What's the world coming to?"

"What kind of bird is it?" says Scarlett.

Mr. Bambuckle smiles. "A blue jay, I should think. I picked him up in Canada."

"Does he have a name?" says Carrot.

"Dodger."

"Dodger is beautiful," I say. "He looks like a jewel."

Slugger calls out from the other side of the room. "Speaking of jewels, I heard there's a jewel *thief* in town!"

"I beg your pardon, dear Slugger?" says Mr. Bambuckle.

"A jewel thief. In town. Someone robbed the jewelry store last night."

"I bet it was Leroy Slip," says Sammy. "The police *never* catch him. He always gets away."

"Leroy Slip is the ultimate escape artist," says Vex, a dreamy look in his eye. "They say he is addicted to two things: fine jewels and large cakes."

Ren's eyes have gone misty too. "A jewel thief?

In Blue Valley? It sounds like the perfect case for me to solve…"

Mr. Bambuckle allows a moment's silence. "This doesn't sound like a case that needs solving," he says. "It sounds more like a case that needs *catching*."

He looks at me and taps the side of his nose.

☆ ☆ ☆

My brother, Toby, will be turning seven on Saturday. Mom and Dad are organizing a party for him. I can hear them talking about it now. I hope they don't invite the McHagils again. Last time Harold's mother came to our house, she brought haggis balls with her. They made the Toddler Brigade spew all over our living room, all over our dining room, and all over pretty much every other room in our house. Apart from my bedroom. I always keep the door locked when I know the Toddler Brigade are around.

I've decided to buy Toby a bike. He has been hounding Mom and Dad for one for months. He can be a little bit annoying at times, but he's family, and Mom and Dad taught me that family is important.

I've also decided to go through with my idea.

*Bake a cake large enough to hide your little brother's birthday present—a new bike!*

I close my workbook and put it in my bag. I'm glad Mr. Bambuckle likes my idea. I hope Mom and Dad do too.

I race downstairs to share my plan. "A bike will be the perfect gift," I say. "Toby's wanted one for a long time."

"You're a lovely sister," says Mom. "I think it's an excellent idea, and it will finally stop him from pestering us!"

"I'll help you make the giant cake," Dad offers.

Mom shakes her head. "I'm afraid we don't have any cake pans big enough for something like that."

An idea pops into my head. "What about one of those novelty cake shops?" I say. "They sell enormous cakes that people can fit inside."

Mom's face lights up. "Of course!"

☆ ☆ ☆

Dad is humming. He's in a good mood. "I've been doing some research," he says.

"About what?" I ask.

He lowers his voice so that Toby can't hear. "Novelty cakes. Big ones. I've put an order in."

"Thanks, Dad!" I whisper. I give him a mini high five.

"Now it's over to you," he says. "You need to find out what kind of bike Toby wants."

"I'm on it," I say.

Toby is in the living room watching television. He has the news channel on. I sit down next to him and pat him on the arm. "Hey, awesome little brother," I say.

"Hey, awesome big sister," he says. Cute.

"You know that bike you've always wanted? What color is it?" I know he'll say "blue."

"Pink."

"Really?"

"Yep. Hot pink."

I am genuinely surprised. "Okay. And what features do you want?" I know he'll say "lots of gears."

"A bell."

"Really?"

"Yep. A loud one."

I am genuinely surprised again. I try for a third question. "Leather seat, right? You've *always* said you wanted a leather seat." I know he'll say "yes."

"No. I want spoke beads."

"Really?"

"Yep. I want lots of spoke beads that pop like cap guns when they bang into each other."

Sometimes my brother surprises me.

A voice on the television distracts me. "There has been another robbery in Blue Valley today."

I nudge Toby. "Can you please turn it up?"

"This morning, Blue Valley Bank was robbed of over a hundred thousand dollars in cash, gold, and jewels. This follows the burglary yesterday at Blue Valley Jeweler's. Police have yet to make any arrests, though it is believed they are closing in on a suspect."

*Interesting.*

Dad pokes his head around the corner. "Victoria, do you mind coming to the kitchen? There's something I'd like to talk to you about."

I know Dad wants to ask me about Toby's bike, so I string him along for a while. "What do you need to talk to me about?"

"Oh, just some things," he says, trying to play it cool.

"Like what?" I say.

"You know...*things!*"

"What kind of things?" says Toby, who is now interested.

Dad is starting to frown. "Things *Victoria* and I need to talk about."

"Can't we discuss it here?" I say. I like teasing Dad.

"No, we need to discuss it in the kitchen."

"Can I come too?" says Toby.

Dad is cracking. "Victoria Goldenhorn, come to the kitchen right now, please! Toby, you stay put and watch television!"

I join Dad in the kitchen, and he laughs when I tell him I was only kidding. "You're too clever for your own good," he says. "Now, what did you find out about Toby's dream bike?"

I tell him about Toby's wish list.

"He's a funny kid, that brother of yours," says Dad.

"I'll go shopping after school tomorrow," I volunteer. "The bike shop is open on Friday afternoons. I checked the website."

Dad is becoming even more excited about our plan. "Perfect! Then, once you've bought the bike, you can take it to the cake shop, and they can put it inside the cake."

"I'll ask them to deliver it on Saturday morning," I say. "Just in time for the party."

"The timing will be tight," says Dad, "but it's worth it."

I walk into the bike shop, holding a wad of ten-dollar bills. I had to break open my piggy bank, but family is worth it.

There are rows of bikes lined up along the floor of the shop. There are even bikes hanging from the walls and roof.

I make my way over to the children's selection and find a hot-pink BMX. It has a basket on the front and ribbons hanging off the handlebars.

"That's our most popular model for girls," says a shop assistant behind the counter. She steps out and wheels the bike to the middle of the floor.

"It's for my brother, actually," I say. "It's his birthday tomorrow."

"How lovely. Does he want any extras?" says the lady, gesturing toward a glass display.

"Spoke beads and a bell, please."

The lady unlocks the display case, and I choose a large silver bell and some metal spoke beads.

"Your brother must love making noise," she jokes.

I pay for everything, and the lady adds the parts to the bike. "Have a nice weekend," she says.

I push the bike outside. I don't want to ride it. That should be Toby's honor.

The novelty cake shop is only a few blocks away, so it shouldn't take too long to get there. I start wheeling the bike along the sidewalk.

*Ding! Ding!*

*Click! Clack! Click! Clack! Ping!*

*Click!*

*Ding!*

*Clack! Clack!*

The noise is unbelievable.

The clapper inside the bell bounces around, slapping the lip of the bell like a loose tongue. It sounds like somebody is trying to drown pots and pans.

The spoke beads pop like mini machine guns. If I close my eyes, I can imagine someone is cooking popcorn with nuts and bolts. *I* want to bolt. But I have to push the bike steadily. I need to look after it for Toby.

Everyone on the sidewalk is staring at me. They move out of the way as though I'm covered in spiders.

But I'm covered in noise. The bike is too loud. It's annoyingly loud.

*Ding!*

*Click! Clack! Click! Ping! Ping!*
*Clack!*

I hope Toby knows what he's wished for. To stay positive, I remind myself of the joy he'll have on his face when he sees the bike.

I reach the cake shop and push the bike inside.

*Ding! Click!*

The shop clerk is speaking with a police officer. The officer looks familiar. I think he visited our school when Mr. Sternblast organized a field trip to the police station last month. Mr. Sternblast took all the credit, but it was really Mr. Bambuckle's idea.

The clerk hands the police officer a receipt and points to a huge cake sitting near the door.

The officer smiles and leaves the shop. He taps the cake near the door on his way out. It must be made of cardboard, because his tap makes a hollow thud. I think I hear something moving inside the cake, but the clerk is talking to me.

"Can I help you?" he says.

I push the bike closer to the counter.

*Ping! Clack!*

He looks at the bike and raises his eyebrows.

"My dad ordered a cake," I say. "A big one—big enough to put this bike in."

The attendant's eyes shine as he remembers. "Yes, of course! I spoke to your father on the phone just ten minutes ago. Victoria, isn't it?"

"Pleased to meet you."

"Okay, Victoria, everything is ready to go. The cake is in the storeroom. If you leave the bike with me, I'll put it inside the cake for you. Our van will pick it up first thing in the morning and deliver it to your house."

"Perfect," I say.

I head for the door and push it open, relieved to be rid of the bike. As I do, a tapping sound comes from inside the cake next to the door.

I don't think cakes are supposed to do that.

☆ ☆ ☆

It's Saturday morning, and our house is buzzing with excitement. Toby can't stop jumping on his bed. He loves birthdays, especially when it's his own.

"Are you sure there won't be any haggis balls?" I ask Mom.

"Positive," she says. "The Toddler Brigade is safe today."

There's a knock on the door, and I run to answer it. A man wearing a baseball cap has wheeled a huge cake to the door. "Delivery for Goldenhorn," he says.

"That's us," I say.

He pushes the cake into the living room. I think I hear a muffled cough inside the cake, but I can't be sure. Besides, bikes don't cough.

Dad pays the deliveryman, and he leaves.

"Everything is ready," says Mom happily. "Now all we have to do is wait for the guests."

The first guest to arrive is Grandpapa. He is wearing his favorite checkered cloth cap, and his beard is as bushy as ever. I give him a big hug and take him into the living room.

"How's my beautiful granddaughter?" he says. "Has that Damon asked you to marry him yet?"

"Only a hundred times," I say. "He took me to the movies, but that didn't go so well. And you've probably heard about the wedding."

"Your mother told me the horrendous details," says Grandpapa, winking. "Speaking of horrendous details, did I ever tell you about the time I was stuck on a sinking battleship?"

I shake my head and sit on the couch next to Grandpapa. I love it when he tells me his stories. I listen closely, because that's what you do with family.

By now, other guests are arriving. Toby has invited his school friends, and they swarm into the living room and start playing video games. Toby cranes his neck to get a better look at the enormous cake.

Soon, our cousins arrive. Mom lures them into the living room with some of her famous cookies.

Finally, everyone is here, and it's time for Toby's special surprise. I give Dad a nod.

Dad stands next to the cake and asks for everyone's attention. "Today is a *very* special day for someone in this room."

Toby can't stop grinning.

Dad winks at the birthday boy. "Someone in this room is about to get a *very* big surprise." Toby's eyeballs are almost touching the cake. "Surprises *don't* come much bigger than this," says Dad.

Suddenly, the lid bursts off the cake, and a policeman jumps out. He looks a little dazed and blinks at the lights. Then he spots Grandpapa. The policeman leaps at him, knocking him off the couch.

"What are you doing?" cries Grandpapa.

"What is he doing?" cries Dad.

"Best party ever!" cries one of my cousins.

Toby is shaking in the corner.

Mom has fainted.

Everyone else is staring, their mouths opening and closing like goldfish.

The officer has Grandpapa's hands in a tight hold. He handcuffs him and flashes his shiny police badge. "You're under arrest for the burglary of Blue Valley Jeweler's and the Blue Valley Bank!"

"I've done no such thing!" says Grandpapa.

"We know it's you, Leroy. We've been tracking you for months."

"But I'm not Leroy. I'm just an old man!" cries Grandpapa. "I'm interested in checkers, reading the newspaper, caramel donuts, and reminiscing—not jewel heists and robberies!"

The officer tightens the handcuffs. "Nice try, Leroy. We finally got you." He pushes Grandpapa toward the front door before adding, "I might even get a promotion out of this."

Grandpapa is whisked outside to a waiting police van. The van skids up the road and disappears around the bend.

Later that evening, Mom is still pale-faced. She plonks a plate of microwave lasagna on my lap and flops onto the couch beside me.

Toby is staring blankly at the television screen. "I didn't ask for a police officer," he says to nobody in particular.

Dad hasn't said much since he returned from the police station. He did manage to explain that Grandpapa is still upset but has been released and is recovering from the ordeal at home. He also mentioned something about Grandpapa demanding that the police buy him a whole box of caramel donuts to apologize. Apart from that, Dad's been quiet.

Something catches my eye on the television. "Toby, can you please turn it up?"

Toby reaches for the remote.

A reporter is standing outside the courthouse. "Despite a bungled trap, police have managed to arrest the criminal behind a recent string of robberies."

Everyone sits up and stares closely at the screen.

"It is believed the police had planned to send an undercover officer—hidden inside a novelty cake—to the criminal's house to catch him with his loot. However, the botched operation saw the cake delivered to an incorrect location, resulting in a false arrest."

The courthouse door behind the reporter opens. A bearded man wearing a checkered cloth cap just like Grandpapa's is led down the stairs by an officer.

The reporter shoves the microphone in the officer's face. "Is Leroy Slip guilty of the recent crimes?"

The officer nods. "That's correct. Mr. Slip has managed to escape our grasp on countless occasions. Today, however, we finally got our man."

Leroy Slip growls at the camera. He looks like a younger version of Grandpapa.

"Well, I'll be," says Dad.

The officer seems to be enjoying the limelight. "Leroy Slip is the master of elusion, but he couldn't fool us this time."

"So how did you manage to catch him?" asks the reporter.

The officer smiles. "With clever planning and some good old-fashioned luck. You see, Mr. Slip has the reputation of being a cake lover. We knew he couldn't resist a large novelty cake. Our officer was hidden inside, ready to catch him with his stolen goods."

"But wasn't the cake with your police officer sent to the wrong address?" says the reporter.

"That's correct. We've since released the man who was falsely arrested. Once we realized our mistake, we immediately sent Special Forces to Mr. Slip's address. That's when things went our way."

"What do you mean?" says the reporter.

"The cakes may have been mixed up, but luck was on our side," says the officer. "There was a children's bicycle inside the cake delivered to Mr. Slip. A birthday present, I believe. Mr. Slip tried to use the bike to escape with his loot when the Special Forces closed in, but there was no way he could escape us on *that* bike. It made enough noise to wake the dead!" He points to something away from the camera.

The camera pans across to another police officer who is loading evidence into a van.

He's wheeling a hot-pink bike. It has ribbons on the handlebars, and there is a basket on the front.

*Ding!*

*Click! Clack! Click! Ping! Ping!*

*Clack!*

Toby stares at the television, and his jaw drops open. "Now *that* is a bike made in heaven!"

# 5

# Questions & Answers

The smell of pancakes wafted through room 12B the following Monday morning as the students took their seats. Mr. Bambuckle, who had watched the news with great interest over the weekend, handed Victoria the first pancake.

"You were right," she said, taking a satisfied bite. "Cake *does* make a wonderful vehicle."

Mr. Bambuckle grinned before passing the plate around the room.

Sammy Bamford straightened his baseball cap and scarfed down his pancake in one mouthful. "Thanks, Mr. Bambuckle!"

Evie Nightingale held her pancake in two hands, nibbling it at the edges. Her eyes darted around the room, on the lookout for any signs of Miss Frost's return.

Slugger Choppers slammed his fist down onto his pencil case in hungry excitement, scattering stationery across the floor.

Victoria, who was thoroughly energized following her cake-related adventures over the weekend, left her desk to pick up the strewn stationery.

Slugger, meanwhile, was already drizzling homemade berry sauce over his pancake, licking his lips in anticipation.

Mr. Bambuckle saved the last crumb of his own pancake and clicked his fingers. Dodger emerged from an inside pocket of his jacket and pecked at the pancake crumb. He chirped his thanks before taking off, disappearing through the door like a blue gem shot from a gun.

"Where's Dodger going?" asked Ren.

"Top secret business, I'm afraid," said Mr. Bambuckle.

"Does Dodger sleep in your pocket?" said Scarlett.

"Wouldn't *you* sleep in a pocket if you found one large enough?"

Evie giggled, then shrank back into her chair at the sound of her own laugh.

"Dodger has slept in my pocket from the time he was an egg," said Mr. Bambuckle. There was a hint of sentiment in his voice. "I found him all alone in a nest in the Canadian wilderness. He had nobody to look after him."

"He must be like family to you," said Carrot. The orange-haired boy knew all about small families, being brought up by only his pop.

"Indeed, he is, my dear Carrot," said Mr. Bambuckle. "But there's something else about Dodger. Something rather peculiar…"

"What is it?" said Vex. "What's peculiar?"

Mr. Bambuckle paused. "I doubt you'd believe me…even if I tried to explain."

The students knew better. They had learned to trust their teacher above all others at Blue Valley School. They pressed him further.

"You can tell *us*."

"We believe you."

"What's peculiar about Dodger?"

Mr. Bambuckle clicked his fingers, and Dodger flew back into the room. The blue jay circled the teacher before resting on his finger, blinking alertly under the classroom lights.

"He's the same color as your suit," said Ren, who was a master at observation.

"And *that*, dear Ren, is the peculiar mystery," said Mr. Bambuckle. "When I first put Dodger's egg into my pocket, my suit was gray. But as soon as his egg hatched, my suit burst into the same color as his feathers. He turned my jacket blue."

While most children would scoff at an impossible story like this, the students in room 12B simply nodded in fascination. Such was their understanding of their teacher's mysterious ways.

Dodger dived off Mr. Bambuckle's finger, vanishing back inside the pocket. The students could have sworn their teacher's jacket glowed just a fraction brighter.

Ren was in detective mode. "Do you ever take your jacket off?"

Mr. Bambuckle thought about this before doing something the students did not expect. "How about I show you?" he said, slipping the jacket from his shoulders and holding it out for inspection.

Vex was at the front of the room in a flash, thrusting his hands into the pockets. He grew increasingly frustrated, turning the jacket inside out in his hasty search. "They're all empty," he said finally. "I can't even find Dodger."

Mr. Bambuckle casually put the jacket back on and reached into the lowest exterior pocket, pulling out a small frying pan. "It's amazing what can fit into a pocket, dear Vex. This is for when I have breakfast alone."

Vex ran his hand through his dark hair in frustration. "But I just checked that pocket! There was nothing in it!"

Mr. Bambuckle smiled at Ren. "I often take it off, dear Ren. How else would I swim in the Amazon?"

"What's the Amazon like?" said Sammy.

For a fleeting moment, the distant sound of drums floated through room 12B.

"Perhaps one day, you'll answer that question for yourself, Sammy," said Mr. Bambuckle.

"Where else have you been?" said Ren.

Mr. Bambuckle paused. "I suppose an easier question would be aimed at where I haven't been."

Ren persisted. "Which is…?"

"Nowhere."

Fifteen collective "Wows" left the mouths of fifteen impressed students. This led to fifteen hands being thrust in the air.

"What's the most dangerous place you've visited?"

"Have you ever been lost?"

"What's your favorite country?"

"Tell me more about the Scottish Highlands!"

"Can you speak any other languages?"

Mr. Bambuckle took a great deal of time answering the questions. He treated each one with enormous respect. His colorful responses—though never exaggerated—expanded the imaginations of the students. The children were in heaven.

Mr. Bambuckle's musical voice filled room 12B for hours that morning. The students—skipping morning recess to stay in the classroom—hung on every word as though each were an invisible treasure.

By the time the lunch bell sounded, the students felt as though they'd returned from an around-the-world adventure.

Before dismissing the class, Mr. Bambuckle scanned the room with thoughtful eyes. He sensed there was more potential in this odd collection of students than there was in any other group he'd ever taught. He opened his mouth to say something, then seemed to change his mind.

"I'm going to the cafeteria today," said Albert Smithers, pulling a coin from his pocket. "Straight after I visit my buddy in the library."

"Your buddy is a maniac," said Vex, stifling a yawn.

"Strong words coming from you," said Scarlett.

"The cafeteria... What a splendid idea," said Mr. Bambuckle. "I think I might join you, Albert. I believe the lovely Carol is on duty today."

"Oh no." Albert groaned. "Cafeteria Carol gave me a microwaved hot dog the last time she served me."

"What's so bad about that?" asked Myra.

"It wasn't microwaved. And it wasn't a hot dog. It was a slab of tofu that wasn't cooked through evenly. Some of it was still frozen hard as a rock, and I chipped my tooth. Then she laughed at me."

"Oh," said Myra. "She gave me frozen tofu once as

well. Luckily, I managed to sell it on as sibling repellent. Nobody likes tofu!"

"Fear not, dear Albert," said Mr. Bambuckle. "I hear the chicken noodles are good this time of year. Come on. Let's go!"

# Conversations with Cafeteria Carol

## CAFETERIA CAROL

## MR. BAMBUCKLE

Not you again.

Delightful Carol, it is so wonderful to see you.

What do you want?

What do you have?

The menu is on the wall. Read it yourself.

A splendid idea, Carol. Though it's a tad far for my eyes to read. Would you kindly pass it here?

Please.

That's correct.

Say "please."

As you wish.

Just say it.

Okay.

What are you waiting for?

You will discover in time, beautiful Carol.

Stop messing around and place your order.

I already did.

Remind me.

I would like a coffee.

I would like a coffee, PLEASE!

Well, I would love to make you a coffee, but I simply don't have the time.

I didn't ask for one.

You said, "I would like a coffee, please."

Argh!

With due respect, lovely Carol, we've been here before. Remember the time you kept ordering chocolate from me when it was I who wanted it from you?

That nearly cost me my job.

Well, we couldn't have that now, could we? Not when you have a reputation to maintain.

What reputation?

The one you have with the students.

I hate the little critters.

They adore you.

No, they don't. They rarely come to the cafeteria when I'm on duty.

I beg to differ. There's a student waiting behind me right now.

I don't care. Just take your coffee and go. I've had enough of you.

Should I not pay for the coffee?

Just take it and go!

You're very generous.

Get out of here!

As you wish. I do hope you'll be as generous with Albert as you were with me.

Who is Albert?

Why, this fantastic young man...

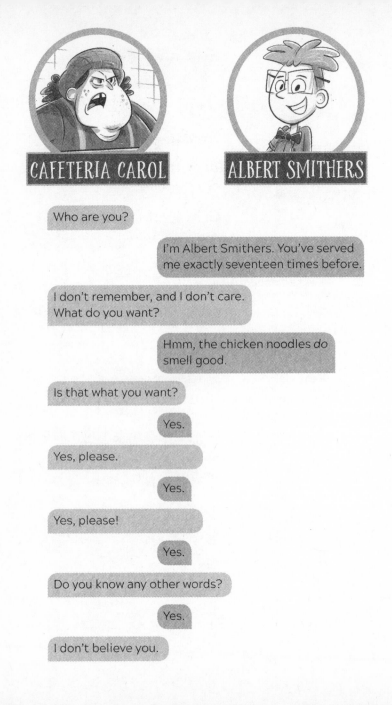

I know all 171,476 words in the Oxford dictionary.

That's just scary.

Do you mean scary in the alarming, horrifying, or spooky way? Or scary in the intimidating, unnerving way?

Who *are* you?

I'm Albert Smithers.

Yes, I know that part!

Well, you *did* ask.

I suddenly remember why I don't like children.

Children are complex creatures, influenced by those entrusted to guard over them and establish scholarly acquirements.

Can you speak English?

I just did. Since we've been talking, I've used almost fifty different English words.

Here, take the noodles and go.
I never want to see another child again.

I've just been to see another child—my buddy. He gave me a present.

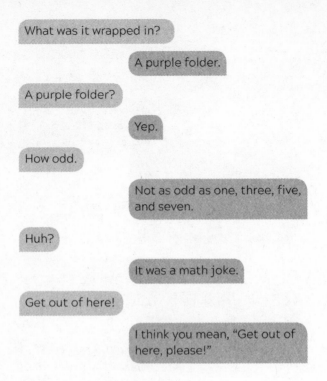

## Buddy Trouble

### Albert Smithers's Story

According to the dictionary—my favorite book aside from *101 Physics Facts That Will Expand Your Knowledge of the Known Universe*—"trouble" means inconvenience and pain, annoyance and agitation, difficulty and distress, and a sense of worry.

This description fits my kindergarten buddy perfectly. Who am I kidding? He's so much worse than that.

My buddy's name is Buster. By my calculations, he's approximately 44.1 inches tall, weighs approximately

47.8 pounds, and causes approximately 309 problems every day. Sometimes that figure is much higher if he hasn't had breakfast, which research suggests is the most important meal of the day. Though this is yet to be formally proven.

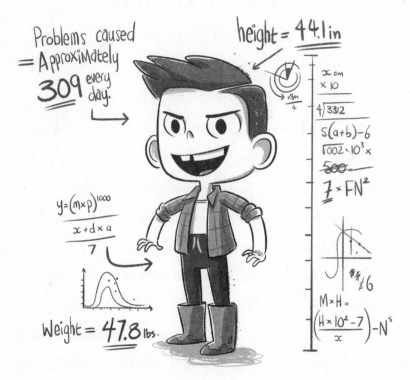

I *have* formally proven that Buster is trouble. I proved it the first day I met him.

Miss Schlump—our class teacher before Mr. Bambuckle—took us down to the kindergarten class-rooms to introduce us to our buddies. The new students were sitting on a mat, waiting for their names to be called.

All of them apart from Buster, that is. He was swinging from a curtain like a smaller, wilder version of Tarzan, throwing pencils at his teacher, Ms. Goss. Some of the kindergarten kids think Ms. Goss is a witch because she wears a cape and has a crooked nose.

Buster leapt from the curtain and landed on a desk. His scruffy brown hair was the same color as the dirt stains on his untucked shirt.

"Get down from there, Buster," demanded Ms. Goss.

"Get down and boogie!" said Buster. Then he started to dance on the desk.

I wondered why Ms. Goss didn't cast a spell on him and turn him into a frog. Maybe she *had* already cast a spell on him and turned him into a devil. But spells are yet to be scientifically proven.

Ms. Goss called out my name and pointed to Buster. "Try to be patient with him, Albert."

"I'll try," I said, though I could feel my heart rate increase by almost thirty percent. Buster scared me. Being patient scared me. The only time I'd ever had to be patient before was explaining negative binomial regression to Miss Schlump.

But my fate had been sealed. Buster was my assigned buddy, and I had an entire year to look forward to spending time with him.

The first thing we had to do with our buddies was show them the outdoor building where the toilets were. "This is the bathroom," I explained.

Buster yawned and scratched his bottom.

I tried to start a conversation with him. "Do you like books?"

"No! Words are for silly Billies."

"Words can help you learn."

"I only like pictures."

"Fair enough," I said. "Anyway, as I was saying, this is the building where the toilets are."

"You're a poo-poo," Buster said.

"Yes, that's what you'll be expected to do in the toilet," I said.

"You're a bum-bum."

"Yes, that's the part of your body that will emit the poo-poo."

"You're a pee-pee."

"Yes, that's also what you'll do in the toilet."

"You're a—"

"I think you should stop now."

Buster pulled down his pants and peed against the wall outside the toilet.

"Couldn't you wait?" I said. "The toilet is literally 8.5 feet away!"

Buster ignored me and continued peeing.

He used it to paint a rude picture on the wall.

"What's that?" I said, knowing full well he had drawn a bottom.

"Your face."

I sighed.

"I like drawing!" he howled, pointing to his master-piece. Or, should I say, master-pee.

Yes, that was quite enough to formally prove Buster was trouble. I simply failed to estimate just how much trouble he was going to be.

☆☆☆

The buddy system was designed by teachers to help ease kindergarten students into school life. No care or consideration was given to the health and safety of the older students.

Buster had been my buddy for about a month, and all he had done was cause trouble.

He had stolen two pairs of my glasses, set fire to a school garbage can, pee-graffitied the toilet wall countless times, destroyed one of my favorite shirts—the one with the picture of Albert Einstein—and swapped one of Slugger's homemade gourmet sauces with radiator fluid. (Slugger was furious and said it tasted disgusting, though later, he admitted his body felt refreshingly cool.)

I tried to take comfort from our science lessons with Mr. Vincent, but all he wanted to do was tell us about the properties of caramel donuts. I was resigned to the fact that my buddy was making life miserable.

"You need to be a better influence," said Miss Schlump. "He's looking to you for guidance."

I wanted to say, "He's looking to me for a punching bag." But I felt nervous, and it came out wrong: "He's punching you like a bloomin' hag."

"I beg your pardon?" said Miss Schlump.

"Sorry, my pituitary gland is sending strong messages to my adrenal gland."

I could tell by Miss Schlump's face that she had no idea what I was talking about.

"He makes me nervous," I said. "I'm even nervous *now* just talking about him."

"Try harder to control him, Albert."

Miss Schlump was not a very sympathetic lady.

☆☆☆

A few weeks later, Buster sent the signals between my pituitary and adrenal glands into overdrive.

"That's dangerous, Buster! Come back!"

Buster had run into the teachers' parking lot, and I was powerless to stop him. The last bell had rung, and the teachers would be returning to their vehicles soon. It was a Friday afternoon, and they were likely to leave in a rush.

"You're a poo-poo," he called from the other side of the parking lot.

All I could do was watch in horror.

Buster strutted along a row of cars and stopped at a bright red sedan. Did you know the word *sedan* is thought to have originally meant "a covered chair carried on poles"? But that's beside the point.

Buster sized up the red sedan with a rather troublesome grin.

It was Miss Schlump's car. Everyone knew which car was hers, because Damon Dunst had crashed it at the car wash fun day. She'd only just gotten it back from the mechanic's.

Buster bent down next to one of the car's tires.

I nudged my glasses farther up my nose to get a better look. "What are you doing?"

Buster ignored me. He unscrewed the air cap, and a hissing noise flowed from the wheel.

"You can't do that!"

"You're a poo-poo."

The tire slowly deflated—much like my feelings about the buddy system—and Buster moved on to the next one.

He let the air out of that tire too—approximately eighty-five percent of it, by my calculations.

Miss Schlump appeared at the far end of the parking lot and started walking toward her vehicle.

I couldn't let Buster get caught. If he got caught, I'd get caught. And I'd be in more trouble than him, because I am the older student and should have been looking after him. Some buddy system!

"Buster!" I hissed. "Miss Schlump's coming." The stress was making my glasses fog up.

I wiped them dry.

Thankfully, Miss Schlump kept glancing at her phone, and she didn't see Buster. She was probably looking at photos of the Swiss helicopter pilot she had a crush on. Everyone knew it was only a matter of time until she followed him to Switzerland.

"Buster! Quick! Get out of there!"

Buster scurried behind another car and gave me a thumbs-up. This made my blood boil, because it wasn't a game. Blood can't really boil, mind you. If it did, you would die.

Miss Schlump got into her car and started the engine. Then she began to reverse slowly. The deflated tires made a horrible flapping sound as she rolled backward. She stopped the car and got out. "What on earth?"

"You're blocking the exit, Schlump!" Mr. Sternblast was jammed in behind her. He beeped his horn.

Another horn honked. Ms. Goss was stuck behind Mr. Sternblast.

Soon, dozens of horns were beeping and honking. Miss Schlump became flustered.

She started jumping up and down like a toddler throwing a tantrum.

Mr. Sternblast got out of his car and stomped over to her. "Snap out of it!" he commanded, holding her shoulders to restrain the tantrum.

Buster squealed in delight and vanished behind some bushes. I didn't see him again that day.

Little did I know, he was just warming up.

☆☆☆

The following week was to be Miss Schlump's last at Blue Valley School. I'm not sure whether the parking lot incident had something to do with it or perhaps her love for the Swiss helicopter pilot got the better of her, but in either case, she handed in her resignation.

"Let's throw a surprise farewell party for her," said Victoria. "That way, we can give her a proper send-off."

"Good riddance, I say," said Vex.

Victoria dug her heels in. "Come on, guys. I know she can be cranky, but at least she's nicer than Mr. Sternblast. Let's give her a happy farewell on Friday."

"Victoria is right," said Damon. His eyes glazed over as he stared at his love. "Let's throw her a party she'll never forget."

It was a party she'd never forget, all right. Never.

☆☆☆

Victoria decided to have the party in the library. Mrs. Paige—who breaks the rules and lets me borrow thirty books a week instead of three—kindly agreed and let us use the main section of the library.

Victoria was in her element. "Ren, you put the ribbons up. Sammy, you pour the drinks. Slugger, you prepare the caviar."

Damon followed Victoria around, echoing her orders. "Ren, you put the ribbons up. Sammy, you pour the drinks. Slugger, you fill the cattle car."

"Prepare the caviar," corrected Victoria. Everything was in place.

The half-time lunch bell sounded, and that was our signal. We hid behind the bookshelves and waited for Miss Schlump to arrive. I sat behind the science books so I could squeeze in a couple of hundred pages of reading while we waited.

Miss Schlump must be a fast walker. I only got through 164 pages by the time she reached the library.

"Surprise!"

Everyone jumped out from their hiding positions and exploded their party poppers.

Miss Schlump put her hand on her heart and smiled.

"Oh, so that's what your smile looks like," said Vex.

Miss Schlump frowned.

"Ah, that's more like it."

"We wanted to thank you for being our teacher," said Victoria. "So we threw you this party."

For the second time in a minute, Miss Schlump smiled.

Then Vex ensured she'd never smile again. "The new teacher is going to be *better* than you, right?"

Miss Schlump crossed her arms. "All I know is that Mr. Sternblast mentioned something about a new, younger teacher who—"

"You're a poo-poo!"

Everyone looked around to find the source of the offensive remark. But I already knew. There was only one kid in school who would say something like that.

Buster had crashed the party. He was balancing on top of one of the bookshelves.

Mrs. Paige was jumping up and down, trying to grab his legs. "Get down this instant!"

Buster dashed along the top of the shelf, sending books flying—at approximately eighteen miles per hour—in all directions. "Words are for silly Billies!" he yelled as a book flapped dangerously close to Mrs. Paige's curly-haired head.

"Albert, control your buddy," cried Miss Schlump.

"But I can't—"

"Just deal with it!"

Buster spotted the party food and leapt down from the bookshelf. He dodged Mrs. Paige's clasping hands and ducked between her legs.

"Get back here!"

He darted toward the food table and snatched the first thing he saw—the caviar.

"No!" cried Slugger.

But it was too late. Buster had already hurled a handful down his throat.

Slugger's face turned red. "I spent ages preparing that, you gourmet wrecker!"

Buster, half choking on the salted fish eggs, poked his tongue out. "You're a pee-pee."

Slugger clenched his fists.

Miss Schlump stepped in to calm things down, only to be met by a spray of fish eggs. Buster had spat out the caviar. "Gross!" he cried.

"My caviar!" Slugger lunged at Buster. But Buster was too quick. He dived under the drinks table. Slugger roared and slammed his arms down on the edge of the table, sending the drinks catapulting over his head. Cups of punch crashed into the shelves, painting the books in red, green, and orange.

Mrs. Paige shrieked.

Mr. Sternblast, who was passing by outside, heard the cry and burst through the door.

Buster took the opportunity to squeeze past the principal to the freedom of the playground.

Slugger took the opportunity to chase Buster, only to barrel into Mr. Sternblast, sending him flying back through the door.

Mr. Sternblast landed outside on a bed of grass. Approximately 943 blades, by my calculation.

Slugger landed outside on a bed of Mr. Sternblast. Approximately one piece, by my calculation.

"Saturday detention, Choppers, first thing tomorrow!" thundered Mr. Sternblast. "And if it wasn't for the fact that your parents donated the new school kitchen, I'd have you expelled!"

Meanwhile, Miss Schlump had seen enough. She stepped delicately over Slugger and Mr. Sternblast, then marched all the way to her car—the red sedan with newly pumped tires.

"I don't think we should expect a postcard from her," said Vex.

Mr. Sternblast stood up, brushing about forty-six blades of grass off his suit. His balding head glowed like lava, and his moustache trembled as though it were about to erupt. "*Who* is responsible for all this commotion?"

Vex pointed at me. "Albert can't control his buddy."

Mr. Bambuckle first arrived at Blue Valley School approximately 4,080 minutes later. It was a Monday morning, and he was balancing on a unicycle on top of his desk, singing us a Mongolian welcome song. I knew right away we would get along well, so I decided to talk to him at morning recess.

"I'm sorry to interrupt you, Mr. Bambuckle," I said. "I know you're trying to order our stickers and stamps, but this is important."

Mr. Bambuckle closed his laptop and winked at me. I could tell by the way his green eyes shone that he was happy to see me. "What can I do for you, dear Albert?"

"It's about my buddy."

"Ah, yes, the infamous Buster."

"How do you know about Buster?"

"I know everything."

I was impressed. It would take an average adult about seven weeks to read through every file at Blue Valley School (five weeks if you took away Buster's).

"I don't know what to do about him," I said. "He causes trouble wherever he goes."

"What do you know about sodium?" said Mr. Bambuckle.

"I don't understand," I said. It felt odd for me to say that.

"Sodium. What do you know about it?"

"Chemical or nutrient?"

"A most wonderful response! The chemical element, if you will."

I thought back to some books I'd read. "Sodium is a very soft metal. Its periodic table symbol is Na, and its atomic number is eleven."

"Very good!" Mr. Bambuckle clapped his hands. "Now, tell me, Albert," he added, "what happens if you drop a piece of sodium into water?"

I paused. "It explodes, of course. Big time."

Mr. Bambuckle opened his laptop and clicked on a link to a sticker website. "That will be all, dear Albert."

I walked out of the room, thinking hard. It was nice to have a teacher who could plant tricky clues in my mind.

By the time I reached the playground, I'd figured it out. It was as though a blindfold had been lifted from my eyes.

Buster was like a piece of sodium. Other people were like water. When you mixed the two—Buster and other people—*boom!*

It was true. All Buster wanted in life was to stir up trouble and make people react. To make them explode. All *I* needed in life was a way to distract him.

☆ ☆ ☆

I'm standing at the edge of the visitors' parking lot, waiting for Buster to get out of his mom's car. He is approximately seventy-five seconds late, based on the weather and local traffic conditions.

Buster opens the door and waves at me. He bounds over and puts something in my hand.

It's a book.

"You're a poo-poo," he says, though I know he's only joking.

"Did you like it?" I say.

"The words are for silly Billies," he says. "But I loved the pictures!"

I take a different book out of my bag and give it to him. "Wanna meet in the library at lunch?"

Buster grins and runs off.

I'm finding it hard to keep up with him.

We've gone through almost every book in the school library, and he's nearly halfway through my collection at home.

It's the pictures. Buster loves pictures.

After the incident at Miss Schlump's farewell party, Buster and I had to help clean the library. It was then that I noticed his attraction to the pictures in the books we had to put back on the shelves. The artworks entranced him. It was like a whole new world had been opened up to him—one where the words played little part.

These days, Buster flicks gently through any book he can get his hands on, poring over the illustrations, tracing them with his finger. Books are the distraction that stops Buster reacting with people. There hasn't been an explosion for weeks.

I hear a shrill cry come from Buster's car. His mom is wrestling with someone in the back seat. It's his little sister.

"Stop tearing at the seats," I hear Buster's mom say. "You're an absolute terror!"

There is another shrill cry, and a doll's head flies out the open door. It soars in a perfect curve, and I catch it in my left hand. There are little teeth marks covering the doll's face.

A banana peel flies through the back window of the car and lands on the sidewalk. A kid in second grade slips on it and lands on his funny bone, which is actually his ulnar nerve.

There are hoots of laughter coming from inside the car. The headless body of a doll somersaults out the open door and is run over by a passing car.

"Bertha!" says Buster's mom. "You're even worse than your brother was at this age!"

I wonder if Buster's mom has formally proven this.

Buster arrives at the library with a purple folder tucked under his arm. He is 132 seconds early, which is good, because I want to go to the cafeteria with Mr. Bambuckle and try the chicken noodles.

"What's that?" I say, pointing to the purple folder.

"A present."

"For me?"

Buster smiles and hands me the folder. His cheeks flush in a cute way.

"Thanks," I say, and I open it. There is a beautiful picture inside. It takes my breath away. "This must have taken you ages."

Buster nods. "Almost a whole week. I worked on it every night before bedtime."

Buster has drawn a lake at sunset. The sun casts golden light over the water. The ripples and waves are drawn in soft, delicate strokes. The yellow tones in the water paint a picture of calm.

"Thanks again," I say. "What's it called?"

Buster giggles and turns for the door. "Lake of Pee-pee!" he cries, running for the exit. "Lake of Peeeee-peeeee!"

# 6

## Things Are Going to Change

With the taste of Cafeteria Carol's chicken noodles still fresh in his mouth, Albert stood proudly at the front of room 12B, holding Buster's artwork above his head for all to see. The picture had inspired him to share his story, and he felt wiser having told it.

"What did you say the drawing was called again?" said Vex, who simply wanted to hear Albert say "pee-pee" once more.

Mr. Bambuckle chuckled. "You, dear Albert, are a rather fine teller of stories. What a marvelous way to commence our afternoon session."

Albert's cheeks flushed with pride. "It must be all the reading I do."

"I'm certain that helps," said Mr. Bambuckle, "though telling your own story is quite a different ball game."

"What ball game?" said Sammy, who was dreaming of playing soccer.

"What's *your* story, Mr. Bambuckle?" said Vinnie White, winding a brown curl of hair around her finger.

"Yeah," said Ren Rivera. "We know that you've been to lots of places, but where are you *from*?"

"Stop wasting time with pointless questions!" said an impatient voice at the door. "You should be learning algebra." It was Mr. Sternblast.

"Dear Mr. Principal, please, come in," said Mr. Bambuckle.

Mr. Sternblast strode to the front of the room with fire in his steps. "Listen up," he barked. "I have some important news."

The students listened closely.

"There's going to be a crackdown. We can't allow classes like this to continue with such airy-fairy nonsense lessons. I'm bringing in someone to help me clean up this school for good. I'm bringing in someone who will boost our grades. I'll get that promotion if it's the last thing I do! Things are going to change, and discipline *will* be the new order!"

Miffy dared to raise her hand.

"Yes, Armstrong?"

"I don't understand. What are you talking about?"

Mr. Sternblast narrowed his eyes and glared around the room. "I haven't forgotten the little stunt that someone in this class pulled." He looked at Scarlett. "You can't get rid of good teachers like Miss Frost in *my* school without consequences. It cost me a better job with more pay. I don't know how you did it, but I'm sure it was *you*. Be warned—all of you! Things are about to change around here, and you're not going to like it. Not one little bit!"

Miffy wished she hadn't asked.

"Now where's that wretched teacher of yours?" said Mr. Sternblast. "He was here a moment ago… This crackdown can't come soon enough!"

The storeroom door at the back of the classroom opened, and Mr. Bambuckle stepped out, holding a brightly-colored glass teacup. "Would you care for some Himalayan tea, dear Mr. Principal?"

Mr. Sternblast spat his response. "I don't drink with my enemies!" He stormed back through the door, his words lingering like a bad smell.

Comforted by the reassuring presence of Mr. Bambuckle, Scarlett stood up and walked to the front of the room. The eyes of her classmates followed her, looking on not with judgment but with fondness and understanding. "I want to say sorry," she said bluntly.

Mr. Bambuckle stepped back and sipped his tea, allowing the conversation to take its own course.

"Why are you apologizing?" asked Victoria.

"For making Mr. Sternblast angry," said Scarlett.

"I'm so glad we have Mr. Bambuckle back, but I don't want our class to be picked on for what I did."

Sammy Bamford laughed in gentle support. "Mr. Sternblast is angry all the time. It's not your fault. Besides, he's always picked on us."

"But this is different," said Scarlett. "*I'm* the one who made Miss Frost disappear. *I'm* the reason Mr. Sternblast didn't get the other job. And *I'm* the reason he hates us so much."

Albert stood up. "And that makes you remarkable, Scarlett. Don't you get it? You did something truly brave. *You're* the reason Mr. Bambuckle is back. *You're* the reason we're learning so much. And *you're* the reason wonderful things are happening to us."

Mr. Bambuckle took another sip of his tea. Beneath his sparkly blue jacket, his heart beat a fraction louder.

"That's right," said Harold. "You and Vex and Victoria made things fun again."

Vex managed a half smile, though his sacrifice of

working long hours in his father's car lot was beginning to take its toll. He rubbed his eyes and rested his head on the desk, pretending to scribble on a piece of paper.

Scarlett was overwhelmed with the feeling of support from her classmates. She tightened the red ribbon in her hair, then clasped her hands to her chest. "You're really not angry at me?" she said.

"Of course not!" sang a chorus of voices.

"We can handle whatever comes our way," said Carrot. "As long as we stick together."

Mr. Bambuckle's heart beat louder again. The students were beginning to band together. This, he knew, was the first step in unlocking their true potential.

Vex raised his head and yawned. "Yeah, yeah…lovey-dovey." His joke was light, but it couldn't hide the dark rings that were appearing under his eyes.

"Lovey-dovey!" Slugger burst out laughing and slammed his hand onto his desk, cracking it through the middle. "Oops."

"LOL," said Sammy.

Carrot sighed.

A flash of blue darted in through the open window and circled the room, chirping brightly.

"Dodger!" cried Myra.

The blue jay flew swiftly into Mr. Bambuckle's pocket, vanishing in an instant.

"Where was Dodger?" said Ren. "What was he doing outside the classroom?"

"Dear Ren, as much as I would love to tell you, I simply cannot at this time."

"Dodger makes such great entrances," said Miffy.

"Which reminds me," said Mr. Bambuckle, "for homework tonight, I would like you all to come up with an imaginative way to enter the classroom."

**Name:** Vinnie White

**Entry:** Walk in normally, sit down normally, take your books out normally, look at your teacher normally, then let out the loudest cat meow you can muster. If you get any weird looks, lick the back of your hand and sniff the air.

**Name:** Damon Dunst

**Entry:** Wear dark gray clothes and pretend to be your teacher's shadow. Lie on the floor and wiggle awkwardly so it looks like you're mirroring their movements. If that's too much effort, simply walk in singing a romantic song to your sweetheart.

**Name:** Albert Smithers

**Entry:** Teleport yourself in using advanced technology.

**Name:** Slugger Choppers

**Entry:** Smash through the wall on a giant wrecking ball. Jump off at the right time and land in your seat (if it's still there). Note: Not for the super-squeamish type. Note for Mr. Bambuckle: I used a hyphen!

**Name:** Miffy Armstrong

**Entry:** Somersault in like a Cirque du Soleil acrobat. Do a triple backflip with a twist and land perfectly in your chair. It sounds hard, but it's really quite easy.

**Name:** Sammy Bamford

**Entry:** Catch an airplane and skydive from twelve thousand feet. Open the parachute and steer it toward the classroom, landing on the roof. Crawl in through the air-conditioning duct and slide out of a hatch positioned directly above your desk. Land silently in your seat before anyone notices.

**Name:** Victoria Goldenhorn

**Entry:** Wear a pointy hat and dive into the room like an arrow. It beats riding a noisy bike!

**Name:** Harold McHagil

**Entry:** Never leave. Camp inside the classroom. Every night. Every weekend. Build a little campfire. Roast marshmallows. Go fishing in the bathroom sink. Use your

desk as a backup shelter. Hang your dirty washing over the desk. Go to the toilet in... Oh, that's kind of a problem.

**Name:** Peter Strayer

**Entry:** Don't enter the classroom. Be somewhere else.

**Name:** Myra Kumar

**Entry:** Enter the room on a giant water-slide. Charge your friends a dollar each to have a turn. Make tons of money and retire early. Move to San Diego and spend your days reading books by Tim Harris.

**Name:** Scarlett Geeves

**Entry:** Sit on an extra-large paper airplane and have a friend toss you through the open window. Do a couple of loops and crash-land on your desk.

**Name:** Evie Nightingale

**Entry:** Being small has its advantages. Disguise yourself as a piece of dust and float in with other pieces of dust. Try not to get stuck in anyone's eye. Being blinked out is not much fun.

**Name:** Carrot Grigson

**Entry:** Saw a hole through the roof and ride a giant pigeon to your desk.

**Name:** Vex Vron

**Entry:** Dig a tunnel from the playground to the classroom and pop up under your desk. This will also provide you with a place to nap and allow quick access to the playground at lunchtime.

**Name:** Ren Rivera

**Entry:** Paint yourself the same color as the classroom wall. Once camouflaged, wait until everybody else comes in, then slowly peel yourself off the wall and take your seat as if it were a completely normal thing to do. Note: Take as long as you like before you peel—good detectives never miss an opportunity to spy!

# 7

## Secret Business

To lighten the mood the following morning, Mr. Bambuckle suggested the students act out their imaginative entrances—as best they could, of course.

Miffy Armstrong went first, executing her backflip with grace and poise. "It's truly not difficult," she said with a bow.

Slugger attempted to copy Miffy's move, which resulted in him landing headfirst on his chair. The seat made a funny *twoing* noise, and two of the legs buckled forward.

Mr. Bambuckle—quick as a flash—turned the lights out with his bouncy ball. The moment the lights flicked back on, Slugger was sitting upright in his chair, which looked as good as new.

The students were beginning to realize their teacher was capable of truly extraordinary things, and rather than stare widemouthed at Slugger—who was looking a little dazed—they applauded with the joy of familiarity.

Ren Rivera acted out her entrance next, flattening herself against the wall. Her challenge was not so much to camouflage as it was to tame her fits of laughter. "I need to work on my spying technique," she said with a chuckle.

Vex pretended to shovel his way out from underneath his desk, earning more laughter from the class. Although the charade put a smile on his face, the dark rings under his eyes betrayed his exhaustion. He had worked particularly hard the night before and had barely slept. After a big yawn, he rested his head back on the desk.

As only a good teacher could, Mr. Bambuckle was reading the signs and keeping a close eye on Vex. He had been using Dodger to help plan something special for the boy—something that would give him the break he so badly needed. It was a surprise the entire class would benefit from.

Aside from Miffy's acrobatic routine, Peter Strayer's entrance was the most convincing. He had chosen to be absent.

"That was a rather splendid way to start the day," said Mr. Bambuckle. "Now, if you'll excuse me for a moment, I have some business to attend to." He opened an inside pocket of his jacket, and Dodger fluttered to his shoulder. The teacher whispered something to the blue jay, and it swooped through the door and out of sight.

"I wish you could tell us where Dodger keeps flying off to," said Ren. "Does it have something to do with the Indian spark-maker beetle?"

Mr. Bambuckle shook his head. "As difficult as secrets are, they are necessary for surprises, and this one will be best revealed at the right time. May I also remind you that Indian spark maker beetles are incredibly dangerous—not something to be messed with lightly."

"Father's bagpipes are not to be messed with lightly either," said Harold. "His playing is lethal!"

While the class chuckled at Harold's joke, Mr. Bambuckle handed out math textbooks—the thick, heavy type that was filled with thousands of problems. "Don't open these yet," he instructed.

"What are we going to learn about?" asked Albert Smithers.

Mr. Bambuckle surveyed the room. "Our learning today will be most important. I've planned a lesson that will teach you *twice* as much as usual."

Albert licked his lips in anticipation.

Mr. Bambuckle walked around the room and checked that everyone was ready. "You may now open your books."

"They're blank!" said Albert. "What kind of textbook is blank?"

"One that you're going to fill in," said the teacher.

"I don't understand," said Vinnie.

"Children are too often expected to *answer* questions," said Mr. Bambuckle. "Today, you are going to *ask* the questions instead. By writing questions—*asking them*—your brain will work in fast-forward, since you'll need to know the answers too. Once you have filled a page with questions, swap books with a partner and answer the problems in their book."

"I want to partner with Victoria," said Damon, hastily picking up his pencil.

"I want to be left alone," said Vex, yawning again. "I hate math."

"Then I shall partner with you," said Mr. Bambuckle, recognizing a familiar tone creeping back into Vex's voice.

The long hours of hard work after school were bringing out more of Vex's brashness. This, the teacher knew, could lead to the boy slipping back into his rebellious ways. He simply couldn't allow it to happen. Not when Vex's sacrifice was the reason behind his return to room 12B, and certainly not when he had so much work to do with him—and the other fourteen students, for that matter.

An hour passed, and the students were steaming ahead with their math.

"We *really* are learning twice as much," said Albert, his face beaming. "Well, 215 percent to be exact."

"Why twice as much?" said Carrot, who was rather enjoying the lesson. "We've never had to learn *twice* as much before."

"Because," said Mr. Bambuckle, "you won't learn a thing tomorrow. Certainly not in this room anyway. Outside, though… Well, that is a different matter altogether."

"What do you mean?" said Sammy. "What's happening tomorrow?"

Mr. Bambuckle clapped his hands together. "Dear Sammy, I am trusting you remember certain…computer skills I sent your way?"

Sammy nodded.

"Good!" said the teacher. "Because tomorrow, they'll come in handy."

The students glanced at each other with nervous excitement. This could only mean one thing—something remarkable was about to happen.

# The Typo

## Sammy Bamford's Story

**D**ad yawns and rubs his eyes. "Have you finished with your plate?"

I nod and wipe my mouth with a napkin.

"It'll be early to bed for me tonight," he says, yawning again.

Dad's yawn makes me yawn. Yawns are funny like that. Though I'm glad farting isn't contagious, because he lets one rip.

I pinch my nose. "That smells worse than your cooking!"

Dad must be tired. He doesn't even smile at my joke.

"I had a bad day at work today," he says. "I fell asleep at my desk."

"Oh," I say.

Dad works for the government. His job is to monitor and record any changes made to laws on the government computer system. The job is about as straightforward as kicking a goal from directly in front of the posts.

He looks around the dining room, as if checking that nobody else is listening, which is weird because we're the only ones who live here. "I made a mistake today, Sammy. A big one. Under no circumstance are you allowed to watch television tonight. Or listen to the radio. Or use the internet. Understood?"

I let go of my nose. "But why?"

"And don't ask any questions," says Dad. "In fact, it's probably best that you go straight to bed too."

I'm confused by Dad's behavior, but I let it go and head to my room for an early night.

☆ ☆ ☆

I'm waiting at the bus stop like I do every morning. But something is different. I'm waiting alone. Usually, there are heaps of other kids standing around with me.

I check my watch to make sure I'm not early. I'm not.

A car swerves past. It's traveling dangerously fast.

A motor scooter whizzes by soon after, and the driver is having trouble reaching the handlebars. The scooter wobbles out of control before eventually crashing into some bushes farther down the road.

The front door of the house opposite the bus stop slams shut. A little girl marches up to the car in the driveway. "I'm ready for my lesson now, Mom!"

A lady—still dressed in her bathrobe—thunders down the driveway after her daughter. "Get back inside this instant! It's time for school!"

The girl crosses her arms. "You can't tell me what to do anymore! I saw it on television!"

Just as things are getting interesting, the bus rumbles around the corner. I pull out my bus pass and step up to the curb. The bus skids to an abrupt halt, and the doors fly open.

I can't believe it.

Slugger is driving the bus!

"What are you waiting for? Hop in," he says.

I step onto the bus and rub my eyes. It *really* is Slugger. He's sitting in the driver's seat with a coffee in one hand. He takes my pass with his other hand and quickly inspects it. "All right, on ya get, buddy. But keep it down. You kids need to remember I have to concentrate."

There are only a handful of other children on the bus.

Too stunned to say anything, I sit down in front of a girl from one of the big schools in the city. She catches the bus every day, and we often talk about sports together. But today, something isn't right.

"Why are you dressed in a suit?" I ask.

"Sorry, can't chat now." She picks up her phone. "Dermot, it's me, Sasha. Sell the Triton Tech shares and invest in Canly Candy. Sell, sell, sell!"

I scratch my head. Something strange is going on.

The bus passes a construction site. A young boy is trying to control a jackhammer. He bounces around like he's on some kind of hyperactive pogo stick. There is a girl driving a digger. She accidentally reverses it into a wall, sending bricks flying out the other side.

What is happening?

The bus jerks. Slugger mutters a word my dad says when his football team loses. To distract himself, he turns up the radio to one of those talk shows that only old people listen to. The host is talking about boring government stuff. Something about new rules. It's the last thing I want to listen to, so I put my headphones on.

Even with my ears covered, I can still hear Sasha yelling on her phone. "Buy, buy, buy!" She is telling someone else to invest in Canly Candy.

The bus stops outside Blue Valley School, and I stand up to leave. "Aren't you coming to school, Slugger?"

"Nah, kid. No time for that. I've got six more runs to do today. Cool, huh!" He waves me off the bus and closes the doors.

Blue Valley School is like a ghost town. Apart from the teachers, who are scrambling around in confusion, I can't see anyone. Where are all the other students?

Then I notice Mr. Bambuckle waving at me from our classroom window. Boy, am I glad to see him. I run over to the room like it's the Olympic one-hundred-meter sprint final.

I'm sitting at my desk. Mr. Bambuckle is riding his unicycle around the empty room. He's cooking an egg and two strips of bacon in his frying pan and singing the Mongolian welcome song.

I look around, confused. I'm the only student here.

Mr. Bambuckle stops singing and flips the bacon. He balances perfectly on his unicycle. "Well, dear Sammy, I suppose you're wondering where everyone is."

I nod. "What's going on?"

Mr. Bambuckle pauses. "Sometimes, those closest to the problem end up being the furthest from it."

"What do you mean?"

"Dear Sammy, did your father allow you access to any media last night? Internet? Television?"

"No."

Mr. Bambuckle looks thoughtful. "Just as I suspected. It seems the good man is protecting you from what he feels may be...*embarrassing*."

"Embarrassing?"

"Personally, I don't think it's embarrassing at all. I think you're missing out on some jolly good fun! But that's just *my* opinion."

"Please, Mr. Bambuckle," I say. "What's happening?"

Mr. Bambuckle, as only Mr. Bambuckle can, sees

the urgency in my eyes. He steps off his unicycle and clicks his fingers. The unicycle wheels around the room and brushes against the class television before steering itself into the corner.

The television flicks on.

A lady is reading the news. "To repeat this morning's main story, the government has announced a drastic reduction of the legal age. The shock decision means the previous legal age of eighteen has been slashed to eight."

The camera shows an enormous line of children lining up for car and motorcycle licenses.

The screen flashes back to the newscaster. "There have already been a number of accidents this morning, and we urge *all* drivers to take care. And now, to other news: shares in Canly Candy are skyrocketing—"

Mr. Bambuckle throws his orange bouncy ball at the television, and it turns off. The ball shoots back and zips into one of the inside pockets of his blue suit.

I look at Mr. Bambuckle and remember my dad's

words from the night before: *I made a mistake today, Sammy. A big one.*

"It was my dad, wasn't it?" I say.

Mr. Bambuckle is honest. "Indeed, it appears he may have made a slight error on the computer system—a typo, if you will."

"What did he do?"

"My guess, dear Sammy, is that he forgot to type a one in front of the eight. It seems eight-year-olds now have the same rights as eighteen-year-olds."

"Will Dad get in trouble? I don't want him to lose his job. He's the only one who can look after me."

Mr. Bambuckle offers me a piece of bacon. "It's never too late to right a wrong, Sammy."

I hear car horns blasting in the distance. I don't want to imagine what's happening. "It's bananas out there," I say.

"It most certainly is," says Mr. Bambuckle with a reassuring smile. He is always so calm.

But I want answers. "How can I fix it? How can I help Dad keep his job?"

Mr. Bambuckle's smile turns mischievous. He rubs his hands together and looks around the empty room. "Well, Sammy, the solution you're looking for is not in *here*."

"Where is it?"

He points to the window. "Out *there*, of course."

☆☆☆

I'm standing outside the entrance to Dad's office building. There are a lot of people scurrying in and out the front doors. They are frowning and carrying fat folders overflowing with pieces of paper. I look for Dad, but I don't see him. I hope he hasn't been fired already.

I try calling Dad on my phone. He's not answering. He's probably inside being yelled at by hundreds of government officials for making such a catastrophic mistake.

I walk up to a guard at the main entrance of the building. He's wearing a black suit and has very short hair.

"Can I come in, please?" I say.

"Nah, kid, government representatives only."

"But my dad—"

"Government representatives only."

I am not one for giving up easily. How else would I win all my running races? "Listen, I urgently need to see my dad because he—"

The guard holds his hand up to quiet me. "Look, kid, you're not getting in."

"I have to see my dad about fixing—"

"It's not happening."

I'm a fast runner, so I try to run past the guard.

He casually sticks out his arm and grabs the back of my shirt.

"I have to get in!" I protest.

The guard spins me around so I am facing him. "There are only two ways into this building, and you're not getting in either of them."

I glance at the busy doorway. There are three more

guards checking the ID cards of everyone who goes in and out. "What's the other way in?" I ask.

The guard laughs. "Forget it, kid. It's a rooftop entrance. No chance." He lets go of my shirt and nudges me toward the sidewalk.

I look up and see a plane flying overhead. It's swaying from side to side like a kite in a windstorm.

A lady holding a pair of binoculars dashes past me, yelling up at the plane. "Be careful, my little dewdrop. Fly straight, fly straight!" She stops running to peer through the binoculars, then holds her hand over her heart.

The plane disappears behind some clouds, and the lady runs after it.

Looking up into the sky has given me an idea. Perhaps the rooftop entrance is my best bet after all.

☆ ☆ ☆

I walk down the main street of Blue Valley, keeping my eyes peeled. I'm probably the only child not driving a vehicle of some kind. A little girl whooshes past me on a motorcycle. She's singing about new rules and no school.

I spot what I've been searching for—a sign in a restaurant window. It says WORKERS WANTED.

I knock on the door, and a kind-faced man wearing a white apron lets me in. He is holding a bowl filled with chopped carrots.

"I'd like to work for you," I say. "I need a job to help my dad save his."

The man looks me up and down. "I'm after a new kitchen hand," he says. "Are you old enough?"

"I'm nearly ten."

The man shrugs his shoulders. "Apparently, that's plenty old enough, nowadays. The job's yours."

"There's just one thing," I say. "I need a cash advance."

The man scratches his head and stares at me for a while before handing over some paperwork. "Sign these, and I'll see what I can do."

I fill out the forms and give them back.

The man takes the paperwork into another room and returns with an envelope full of cash. "I don't usually do this," he says, "but you remind me of me when I was a boy. I like your spirit. That's your first month's pay. You start tonight at six. Don't be late."

I head back out to the main street of Blue Valley. A dairy truck has lost its load, and there is milk all over the road. The driver of the truck—a little boy—is yelling at a man who is standing next to a red car. "It's called a stop sign for a reason, you nincompoop!"

The argument fades behind me as I head to my next stop—a place I have only ever dreamed of entering. Dad used to warn me about going inside. "You have to be eighteen to buy what they sell," he would say.

I push the door open and walk in.

☆ ☆ ☆

Before I leave the shop, I place my supplies into a backpack and very, very, very gently put it on. I keep walking down the main street of Blue Valley to my next stop: rental cars.

There is one car left in the car lot. It's old and covered in dents and scratches.

A lady hands me the keys. "Sorry, it's the only vehicle we have left," she says. "The new laws have been great for our business. You're about the hundredth kid we've dealt with today."

I very, very, very gently take off the backpack and put it on the passenger seat. I clip the seatbelt over it for good measure. You can't be too careful with these things.

The lady walks back through the empty car lot to her air-conditioned office.

I start the engine and press my foot down on the accelerator. The engine roars, but the car doesn't move. I try to remember what I've seen in movies—something about an emergency brake?

I release what must be the emergency brake and press the accelerator again. The engine screams, and the tires skid across the gravel car lot. I screech out onto the main road and turn left, following the signs to the airport.

☆ ☆ ☆

Sometimes I get scared before a big game. My stomach feels as though it's been turned inside out. Miss Frost made me feel like that too.

Right now, my gut is practically doing somersaults, because I'm scared of more than just a game. The first thing that terrifies me is Dad losing his job. The second thing is the fact that I am twelve thousand feet in the air. I suppose you could throw a third in—I'm about to jump out of an airplane!

The pilot—a teenager with pimples—gives me a thumbs-up. I make sure the parachute is strapped securely to my back before I edge closer to the open door. It's so windy, it feels like a thousand invisible hands are slapping me. The previous age restrictions made more sense. Nobody under eighteen should be doing this on their own.

I clutch the backpack very, very, very carefully to my chest. I close my eyes and jump.

My stomach lurches with the sudden drop. All I can hear is wind pounding in my ears.

I hope the backpack is okay. I hold it tightly.

My face feels like it's about to be ripped off.

I can't see, because my eyes are closed.

I open them.

Blue Valley is far, far below. The sports field where I train every second afternoon looks like a little green matchbox. The buildings that line the main street are tiny stamps.

I can just make out the government building where Dad works. That's my target. Somewhere on the roof is a way into his office. It's a doorway to helping him *not* get fired. If he hasn't been fired already, that is.

I feel like I've been fired out of a cannon.

One that's pointing at the ground.

I hold the backpack with one hand and yank the

ripcord with the other. The parachute opens and slows my fall. The wind stops slapping at my face.

The backpack is getting heavy, but I can't let go of it. I hold it tight against my chest with my elbows and use my hands to steer the parachute. I'm heading straight for Dad's building.

The building is getting bigger. It doesn't look like a stamp anymore. It looks like a building. A hard, concrete-roofed building.

Suddenly, the roof of the building is charging up at me. I bend my knees, ready for impact. I land on the roof, half running, half falling, half celebrating. That's three halves, but I don't care. I'm just happy to be alive.

I unclip the parachute and run to the safety of a large air-conditioning duct. I don't want to be seen. Not yet. Not until I've opened my backpack.

I unzip my pack and start unloading the precious cargo. Firecrackers.

Dad's typo meant I could buy them. Hundreds of

them. Small ones, big ones, blinkers, flares, crossettes, sparklers, rockets, and palms.

All unpacked.

All ready to be lit.

☆ ☆ ☆

I crawl through the air-conditioning duct on my hands and knees, placing firecrackers every few feet before wriggling farther along. The firecrackers are connected by a thin metal wire that I unravel as I go.

I occasionally hear snippets of conversations from the offices as I pass over them.

"The children are overrunning us."

"The country's in a mess."

"That Bamford should be fired immediately if he doesn't fix it."

"Other countries are following the trend."

"How could one typo cause so much chaos?"

I place my last firecrackers inside the air duct on the

lowest floor, then quietly crawl back to the fourth floor—Dad's level.

I open a hatch and poke my head through. I can see Dad at his desk, frantically typing away. He is also on the phone, and I can hear the voice at the other end of the line yelling, "You caused this problem, Bamford! You fix it!"

I slide through the hatch and land silently on the carpeted floor. Soccer has taught me to be light-footed.

"Dad?"

He spins around. "Sammy... What are you doing here?"

"I've come to help you. I don't want you to lose your job. You need the money to look after me. To look after *us*."

Dad's face drops. "You know about my mistake?"

I want to laugh. "Everybody knows. It's wild out there."

Car tires squeal down on the street below. A siren fills the air.

"I don't know what to do, Sammy." Dad's eyes are tired. "I've tried everything, but the computer system needs a total override. All I did was leave out a one in front of an eight…"

My moment has come. My life has been building up to this point in time. "I know what to do," I say. "I know how to override it."

"But how—"

"Just trust me, Dad." I sit down at the computer and start typing away.

Those countless lessons in the computer lab. The email links from Mr. Bambuckle. He knew. Somehow, he knew it would help me now. My fingers work hard as I type code even Albert would be proud of.

"Well, paint me red and call me a firecracker," says Dad.

☆ ☆ ☆

Dad passes me a napkin. "Thanks for what you did today, Sammy. I'm glad I still have my job and that things can go back to normal now."

"I'm glad too," I say.

"Tell me again, where did you learn to code like that?"

I wipe my face with the napkin. "Let's just say that Mr. Bambuckle sent me a few pointers."

"He's a clever man, that teacher of yours," says Dad.

We put our dishes in the sink, then plop down on the couch. Dad flicks on the television to catch the end of the news.

"In finance, shares in Canly Candy have crashed after reaching an all-time high earlier this morning…"

Dad laughs. "Don't tell me you invested in that garbage?"

"No. I spent my money on saving your skin, remember?"

"Recapping our main stories," says the newsreader, "the government has dramatically reversed itself on new laws allowing eight-year-olds to have the same rights as eighteen-year-olds. The move comes just twenty-four hours after the controversial change to legislation."

The television shows hundreds of adults dancing in the streets. Fireworks explode out of the government building's air vents, painting the sky in dozens of bright colors.

"Couldn't help myself," I said, looking at Dad sheepishly. "I knew I'd only have one chance to legally buy fireworks before I turn eighteen. Besides, a celebration was in order."

My phone rings.

"Who is it?" says Dad.

"I'm not sure," I say, picking up the phone. "Hello?"

Dad sees my face drop. "What's wrong, Sammy?"

"I'm late for work!" I grab a clean shirt and run for the door.

"Where are you going?" Dad calls after me.

"Like I said—work!"

I slam the door and run outside, jumping onto my bike. I start pedaling for the main street in town.

I'll tell Dad the whole story tomorrow. I'll tell him how I signed papers that mean I have to work to pay off my advance no matter how the laws change.

I'll tell him how I had just enough time to get a tattoo of a soccer ball on my ankle after I bought the firecrackers.

And I'll tell him the worst part.

I'll tell him how I accidentally got the one and the eight mixed up. I'll tell him before he finds out that eighty-one is the new legal age instead of eighteen.

It'll be easy to tell Dad the truth. Because technically, he'll still be a kid.

# B

## Mr. Sternblast's Announcement

The students in room 12B were the only kids in Blue Valley to walk into school with a spring in their step the next morning. Despite the outrageously exciting adventures of the day before, the students knew that their classroom was the real starting point for all things remarkable.

Mr. Bambuckle greeted them on his unicycle, though to their surprise, he wasn't holding his familiar frying pan. Instead, he held out a tray full of mini pizzas. "My dear students, please try one of these rather delicious breakfast pizzas."

"Yum!" said Vinnie.

"Double yum!" said Ren.

"I detect a slight hint of rosemary...and saffron," said Slugger.

"I had a really old bus driver this morning," said Carrot, changing the subject. "He must have been almost a hundred."

"Yeah," said Myra. "The line at the supermarket this morning was unbelievable. The checkout lady had to be at least eighty. She kept asking me if I had exact change— whatever that means!"

Victoria laughed.

"That reminds me," said Damon. "I bought you these." He handed Victoria a bunch of neatly arranged flowers. "They only cost me five dollars."

"I saw an old lady getting a tattoo," said Scarlett. "She was a total punk gran!"

Sammy exchanged glances with Mr. Bambuckle and grinned. "I'll fix it at lunch," he mouthed to the teacher.

Mr. Bambuckle winked and took the last bite of his pizza.

Just when the children finished licking their fingers, an announcement blasted over the school loudspeakers. "Attention, all students, please report to the gymnasium immediately for an urgent assembly." Mr. Sternblast's voice carried a triumphant tone. The students knew this meant trouble.

"Let us not be late," said Mr. Bambuckle, gesturing toward the door.

While the teacher's face showed no sign of fear, he recognized the tone in the principal's voice too. It was enough to stop him sending out Dodger for one final mission. He would simply have to wait before he shared the exciting news with the students.

The students filed through the door and made their way to the gymnasium, followed by their cherished teacher.

Mr. Sternblast was waiting on a podium, tapping his foot impatiently. His moustache was freshly trimmed, and there was a look of victory in his eyes.

The students took their seats and waited.

Mr. Sternblast tapped the microphone. "I have called this assembly to share some important news with you."

Evie fidgeted nervously with her dress.

"The school board has made a decision to help boost the grades here at Blue Valley School. They have elected to permanently appoint an extra member to our staff—one who will be in charge of...*discipline*. With better behavior, we can expect better grades. Discipline is the new order."

Vex stifled a yawn, his curiosity fighting off sleep.

Mr. Sternblast strode over to the door at the side of the stage. "It is my pleasure to introduce you to our new staff member."

A young woman stepped onto the stage. She was dressed in stylish white clothing, and her gray-blue eyes were as cold as a midwinter blizzard. A diamond bobby pin held her silver hair back in a meticulously neat high bun.

Mr. Sternblast rubbed his hands together. "Students,

please welcome back Miss Belladonna Frost—your new assistant principal!"

Miss Frost strode across the stage. Ren Rivera noticed that her nose had gone back to the size noses should be.

"Look at her bobby pin," whispered a boy in second grade.

Miss Frost turned quickly and gave the boy such a frightful stare, he burst into tears.

Only one person in the room responded positively to this bombshell. Mr. Bambuckle's enthusiastic claps echoed loudly throughout the hall. "Bravo! Bravo!"

Miss Frost took the microphone, her icy whisper raising the hairs on the backs of the students' necks. "We start our crackdown in exactly one week's time," she said. Then she sent a particularly piercing stare in the direction of Mr. Bambuckle. "Discipline is the new order."

Mr. Bambuckle couldn't hold back his smile. "How delightful," he said and clicked his fingers. "Exactly one week. Did you hear that, Dodger?"

And with that, the blue jay shot out of his jacket pocket for its final mission.